The Northman's Daughter
3 Books

E. Merwin with Ben Ressler

Copyright © 2005, 2015 Eileen M. Ressler & Ben Ressler
Based on the "The Banshees and the Wild Boar" by Ben Ressler, 2002

Second Edition First Printing 2015 USA. All rights reserved.

This is a work of fiction. Names, characters, places and incidents are products of the authors' imaginations and used fictitiously. No part of this book may be reproduced in any form or by any means, electronic or mechanical, including photocopying, recording or by any information storage or retrieval systems, without the written permission of the copyright owners.

Book Bogglers Collective
www.bookbogglers.com

ISBN-13: 978-0692528525
ISBN-10: 0692528520

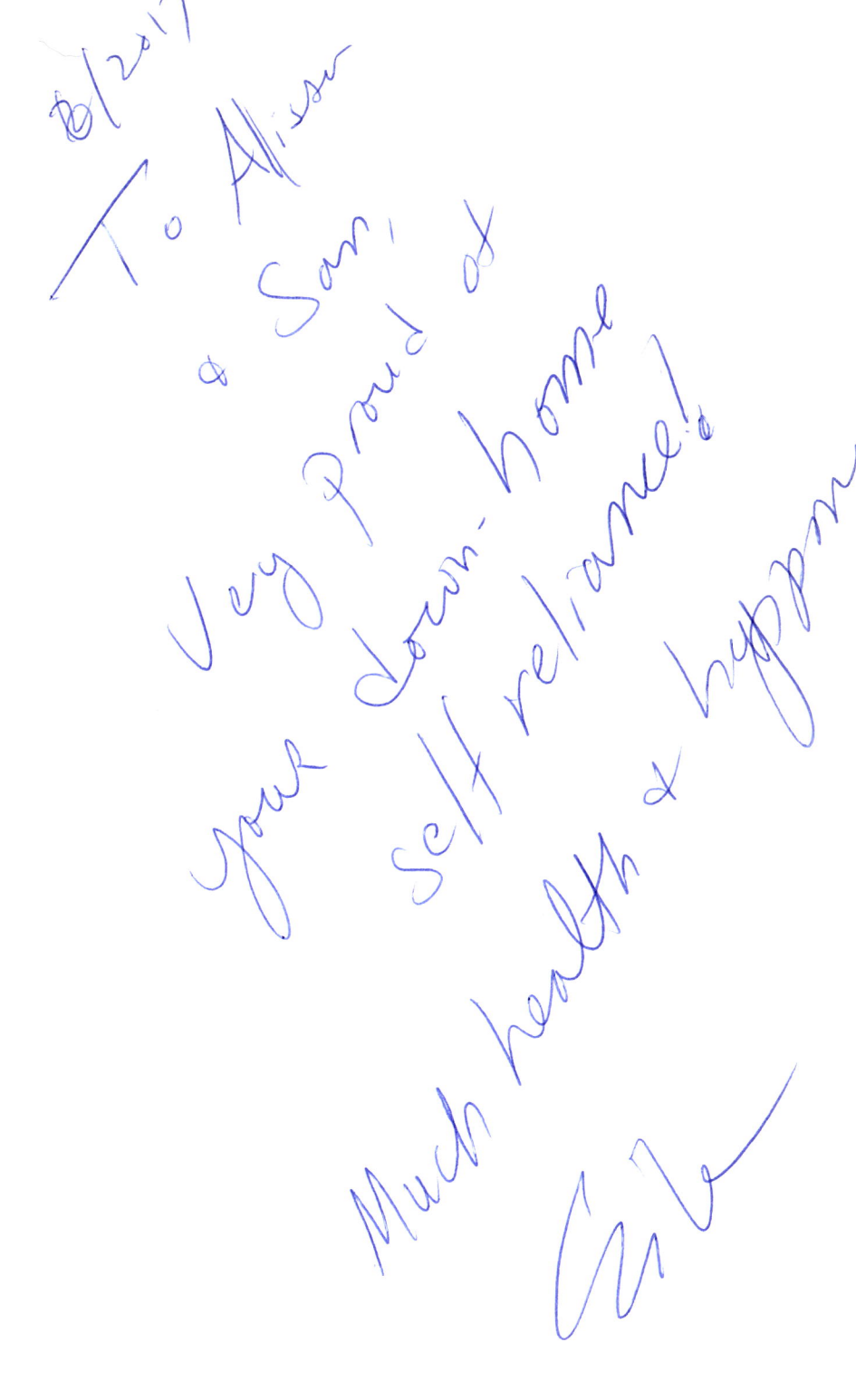

8/2017

To Allison & Sam,

Very proud of your down-home self reliance!

Much health & happiness

Eve

With gratitude to our ancestors &

hope for the generations to come.

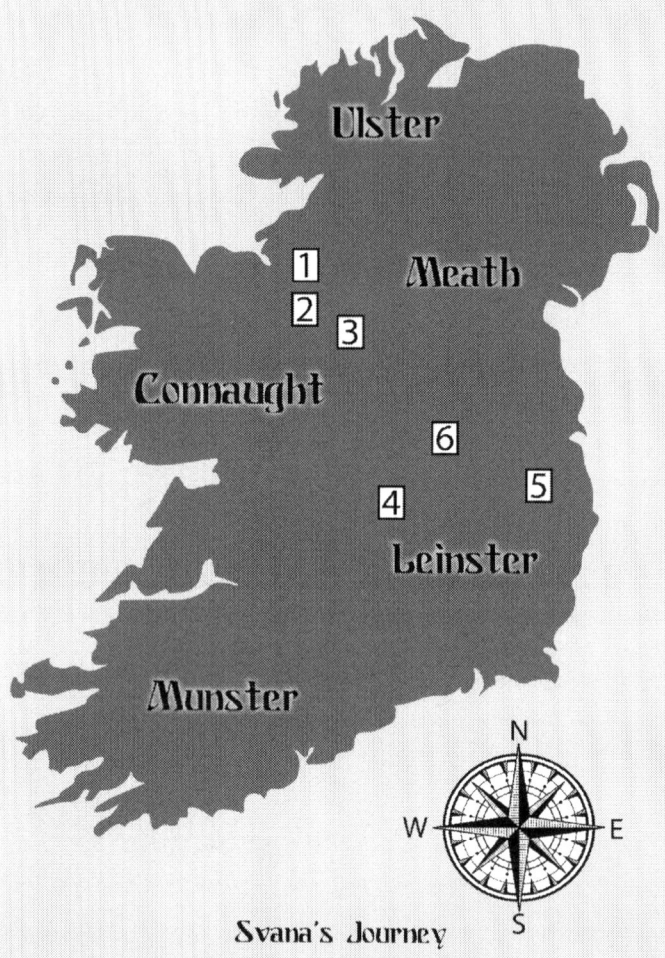

Ancient Ireland

Svana's Journey

1. Knocknarea: site of the Cairn of Queen Maeve
2. The Caves of Kesh-Corran: site of the home of Camog, Skein & Holly
3. Lough Arrow: site of the Battle of the Plain of Tears
4. Kildare: homestead of Finn MacCool
5. Dubh Linn: site of the Viking stronghold
6. Hill of Tara: site of the ancient Irish capital

Contents
Book 1: Floating Bones

Burns...1

The Silver Hand..16

Floating Bones..32

Hill of the Moon...42

Skull..51

Hags of Kesh Corran..58

Book 2: Cauldron of Undry

Cauldron of Undry 71

Crossing Lough Arrow 84

Morrigan's Song..95

Abduction of Sabd 105

Fer Leath...118

The Estate 136

Book 3: Well to Tirnanóg

Scalpeen...146

Bounty..164

Return of Brann 169

Salmon of Knowledge 177

White Sided Tara..187

The Last Guest 203

    Timeline...221

    Glossary...223

    Bibliography 237

    Acknowledgements 238

Burns

The crashing waves rush back to sea as Svana runs along the surf, her bare feet blue from the icy water. The shells of mussels rattle and a lone gull caws from the rocks studded with snails and slick with black green seaweed. Standing on tiptoe, she studies the bird and then caws back, eager for an answer, but the bird spreads its wings and flies off into the gray and brooding sky, leaving her alone again.

From over the hill just beyond the hermit's hut, the village children slide down the grassy dune toward the beach. Svana hides behind the rocks, listening to the wind carry their shouts down the strand. "They're coming, they're coming!" Peeking out, she sees the biggest boy point toward the horizon. "Run, the long ships are coming!" Shrieking with imagined terror, children scatter, echoing his alarm, "They're coming, they're coming!"

Leaping from her place behind the rocks, Svana waves her arms and runs down the beach. "They're coming, the Northmen, they're almost to shore!" The children stop and stare at her approach, her shouts drowned out by the crashing surf.

The gang encircles the child. Motionless she stands at the hub of their hatred, watching the boy scoop up a clump of wet sand and broken shells, molding it between his thick hands. He flings it, hitting her with a stunning blow to the temple before another clod strikes her between the shoulder blades, and she falls to the ground as the children attack striking her from all sides. She draws her thighs to her chest and tucks down her head to hide her bloody face. Around her they circle, chanting, "Burner, burner!"

"I'm not the burner," she cries. "I'm not."

Her muscles flinch with each punch and kick recalled. Though safe on a bed of deerskin hides close by her sleeping grandmother, her heart races, her mind replaying the attack that left her bloody and broken on the cold sand.

Svana stirs and sees the last chunk of turf tumble into ash. From the ring of white stones at the center of the hut, the ribbon of smoke rises through the hole of the wickerwork beehive where she lives with her grandmother far from the village.

Pushing back the cowhide that hangs over the doorway, she crosses to a stack of turf bricks covered with hay. A harsh wind blows off the sea as she brushes back the straws and reaches for the dried clods of ancient earth that warm their hut and cook their food. She carries three inside, and kneeling by the ring of stones, sets them near the dying embers and blows hard to spark a flame before creeping over to the old woman who sleeps with her feet toward the fire.

From her deerskin bed Svana reaches for the blanket that she spreads over her grandmother, admiring its purple color, still rich although twelve years have passed since its making.

"The color, child, is it still true?"

"It's still true, Mamó," she replies, repeating the line she has heard so often, "for you dyed it with a thousand whelks."

"I can remember cracking the shell of each periwinkle your mother and I gathered in our baskets from the rocks down by the sea." The old woman sits up with the memory rising within her. "For days we sat and broke each at the back, picking out the vein with a bodkin until our fingers were sore. Drop by drop the dye trickled into the bowl. Finally we had enough to soak the blanket, woven from the wool of our own sheep until it gleamed with the color of a dark wet berry. Then we hung it over a bush to dry."

Svana tucks the blanket about the legs of the frail woman whose leathery hand runs over its folds, her fingertips seeing what is now dim to her eyes.

"Way off in the village it caught the eye of the Chieftain's daughter who thought it must be a purple gem set in the green hill. Greedy girl, she sent her father to bring her back the jewel. But when his mare trotted up to our doorway, he saw it was a length of wool so expertly dyed, so rich in color that he knew he must have it for his own household."

"But you wouldn't let him have it, would you, Mamó?"

"Wise we were not to sell it that day. For the silver would have long ago been spent, and what comfort would these old bones have had?"

"Tell me again how much he would have paid."

"A *dirna* of silver, and a fine price it was, the price of a cow with calf."

The girl squats beside her, wrapping her thin arms around her knees. "Then what did you tell him?"

"Says I to him, it's but a lowly chieftain you are. This blanket was made for one of higher rank."

"Was he angry?" she asks as if hearing the story for the first time.

"Fit to be tied," cackles the old woman. "For says I to him this blanket belongs to a daughter of the *Tuatha Dé Dannan*, a descendant of the first true kings and queens of all Ireland."

The girl speaks in a deep voice. "I see no signs of royalty in this hovel!"

"Then you've clods of mud in your head where your eyes should be, for she sleeps in the shade of that young rowan tree."

"It's nothing I see but the offspring of insolent hags." The child raises her arm to strike the old woman.

"And I see nothing more than the mud at my feet." The old one's eyes spit back the glow of the turf fire.

"Then what did you do?"

"I scraped a ball of mud and stone into my hands and into it spat an ancient curse and hurled it so hard at his chest, I nearly knocked him off his horse." The old woman chokes with laughter. "It was a sight worth double the silver he'd have given me. Him teetering up there on his mare, his face so red and bloated with the rage that was in him I thought his cheeks would burst like a stuck pig's bladder."

"You showed him, Mamó."

"Aye, *a ghrá*, it was a grand sight indeed."

"And did he leave us alone then?"

"Oh, he tormented me long after, trying to get rent for this hill that he had no more claim on than a hawk circling above a flock of sheep." The old woman's head bounces with a dry, raspy cough.

The child ladles a scoop of boiling water into a thick clay cup and sweetens it with a chunk of honeycomb from the *bechdin* that hangs from the same rowan tree at the edge of their herb garden where the wild bees swarm. She cools it with her breath, then holds the old woman's head and tips the cup to her lips.

"Sure, it's hard times that are on us, child, when we've only water from the well and not even a sup of milk to sweeten."

Gently Svana sets her grandmother's head down on the woolly sheepskin that softens the curve of the small log that is her pillow. From a wooden bowl nearby, she reaches for a rag and wrings out the cool water, setting it on the hot brow of the old woman whose eyes droop. The girl watches and waits until she is sure that the old woman has fallen back to sleep. She then steps from the hut and out into the October night where swirling clouds cross the blue black sky.

Every night she walks the narrow path across the field that leads to the rocky cliff and down to the sea. To her the ocean air is like food and the long strides of her legs as essential as breathing. Her grandmother, having long ago accepted her wandering ways, offers no protest—except twice during the shifting year: once on the night when spring tumbles into summer, then on the eve of Samhain, the night when winter steals back over the land. For it is on these nights when the wall between two worlds crumble, and the spirits from the Other Side step over the rubble to walk freely across the fields and hills of what was once their own beloved island. These are the two nights her grandmother has forbidden the girl to go out, for on these nights a journey begun might never end because any foolish mortal could fall into that phantom world forever.

But being always restless, Svana cannot bear more than a few waking hours confined to the hut. After all, she tells herself, even if spirits do walk with her, why should she fear the dead? All her grandmother's stories are peopled by ancestors who once were great, but now are gone. They are her unseen family, the only family she has ever known: the chieftains, kings, queens and warriors of her grandmother's stories of the Tuatha Dé Dannan.

Often on her nightly walks by the sea, she imagines the horses of her ancestors charging toward shore on the crests of the waves. Once in the swirling foam at her feet, she saw a woman's face appear, entwined with curling strands of windswept hair, but before she could study her features, the wave retreated and the rippled sand at her feet left no trace.

Svana clamors up the rocks slick with seaweed and looks up at the stars. Again she sees the female face in the sky that dissolves into a silver cloud that shifts into another shape, a hand whose finger points eastward. She gazes at the omen until a great wave crashes against the rocks.

For a moment she teeters then squats down to regain her balance, but a second wave crashes over the rocks, sweeping her into the sea. Dragged down into the undertow, she is struggling in the icy blackness when her forehead bashes against a boulder, and she struggles no more, the sea tossing about her limp body before spitting it out onto the shore.

Senseless she lies there, unconscious of the hooded figure who pads down the beach on bare feet to kneel beside her. The man pulls back the folds of the cloak that mask her face then presses hard on her chest until she spits out a gush of grey water and rolls onto her side. Carefully he lifts the slight body in his arms and carries her toward the squat dome of tightly fitted stones where he lives alone by the sea.

He passes the child through the low doorway before entering on hands and knees to place her on a patch of rushes that carpets the bare ground. After a few minutes she stirs and stares at the light and shadows cast by the fire on the curved stone wall.

"Mamó?"

"No, child, though asleep by her side is where you ought to be."

Svana sits up slowly, shivering as the cold strands of sea water run down her skin, and the old man throws back the hood of his cloak, revealing a gaunt face from which his eyes shine like two lanterns set on a craggy ledge.

"Take off that sopping dress and wrap yourself in this before you catch your death." He hands her a tanned hide and sits down on a low stool by the fire with his back turned to the girl who struggles out of the heavy folds of the drenched mantle and peels the linen slip from her back that glistens in the firelight. Wrapping herself in the animal skin, she sits across from him.

His name is Harte. The child is not alarmed to find herself here in the hermit's company for she is well acquainted with this hut. His is the only dwelling beside her own that she has ever entered. Like her grandmother and herself, the hermit lives apart.

"A raw night indeed to be out climbing the rocks."

The hermit leans over the low fire to stir the copper pot that dangles from an iron hook.

"I slipped."

"I can see that by the *mioscán* on your brow."

Her fingers touch the swollen knot that is throbbing with pain.

"Maybe that will teach you to mind your grandmother, but I doubt it."

With a wooden bowl Harte dips into the cauldron and scoops up a portion of steaming soup made from prawns, periwinkles, *duilesc* and seaweed. With both hands Svana cups the bowl, closes her eyes and inhales deeply, welcoming the steam that moistens her face. Then sipping the scalding broth, she feels its heat course down her throat and fill her chest and stomach with warmth. After she slurps the last few drops, she plucks the tender bits of seafood from the bowl and pops them into her mouth, licking her fingertips clean. She puts aside the bowl with a nod of thanks while the fierce wind sweeping off the beach blows a sad note over the smoke hole of the *cloghan* like lips over a clay jug.

"A noisy wind this night."

"Have you no fear as Mamó does of the spirits out riding the wind of Samhain?"

"The only spirit that visits my lonesome hut fills me with hope and joy, and like yourself is always welcome."

"Tell me again why you live alone, Harte."

"Because it is God's will."

"But how can you know the will of the gods when there are so many?"

"Your grandmother still holds to the old stories, and in them there are more gods than kings and chieftains in all Ireland. But be it many or one, there is still a single will that drives this world."

"Is it your god's will that we must live apart from the village?"

"It's not for me to know the will of God as it's only a servant I am to that will myself."

"Then why do you think we've had to live so long apart?"

Harte tightens his lips.

"You do know, Harte, and it's not fair that you won't tell me!"

"Svana, I'm telling you for the hundredth time, that story is for your grandmother to tell, not I."

"But I must know."

"It's like a badger I am with the hound yapping down my burrow."

"But, Harte," she begs. "I've asked and asked, and she'll not tell me but small bits until now she seems so tired, I can't ask her anymore."

"Then let the story rest with her, child."

"But I'll not rest until I know "

"Nor will I with you chattering at me like a magpie."

"So tell me, Harte, tell me so I won't be nagging you or Mamó anymore."

"Aye, for the sake of her rest and my peace, then I'll tell you. But only that small part of the story that was my own."

"I promise I'll not tell."

"Sure, but if that promise is ever broken, I'll know by the sight of her coming over the hill with a crooked stick to beat over my old head. For if that woman is not the living proof that you are born of a warrior race, then the sun itself will turn cold at dawn."

"I swear, I'll not tell her."

"Then this is how it was."

Harte bends forward to stir the soup. From the roiling swirls of seaweed and coils of steam his tale bubbles up before them.

"That afternoon when the women of the village were out gathering mussels on the beach, the jagged helm of a boat dashed to bits washed ashore. They ran for the men, but none could identify the make of it because it was unlike our own hide-covered *curraghs*. It was then the sea spat out a dying man by whose tattered trousers and cropped yellow beard we knew to be a Northman, one of the marauders who not a year before had landed their longboats on shores to the south where they plundered and burned, taking off with them a score of sobbing women and children to be sold as slaves. Some called to kill him on the spot.

'Like the fierce wolves that prey on our lambs in spring, he deserves no less than a spear through his side,' cried one while another declared they should call for the *Brehon* who knowing our laws could best judge his fate.

'Only men deserve fair judgment, and Northmen are no less than beasts.' So they argued the fate of the half-drowned man until one lass took pity on him and shouted in a voice that silenced the others. 'Northman or no, it's still a man that's lying here before us. What say you, hermit? You are a man of God.'

I stepped onto the rocks and cried out over the waves that as men of law we could well afford patience, for if the Northman died that would be an end to it, but should he live, the Brehon would pass judgment on his lot."

"But, Harte, he was a Northman."

"Northman or no, all men must play out the lives given them by God."

"But his people killed our people. The villagers were right, he deserved to die."

"There's far more danger in not forgiving."

"What good can come of letting an enemy live?"

"Svana, trust me. Killing leads only to killing."

"So what did the villagers do?"

"Some grumbled, but most agreed that the fate of the Northman should be left in the hands of the Brehon and his wisdom of our people's law. So they dragged his body into this hut as the cold fists of winds beat against its round wall."

"Did they leave him alone?"

"All but one in the crowd left. And it was she who trickled the hot broth between his swollen lips and tended him in the days to come that saved him. Revived as much by the fire and the food as by the beauty of the lass who nursed him."

Svana picks out a prawn from the wooden bowl and nibbles the last morsel.

"Here, give me your bowl." Harte dips it again into the steaming cauldron.

"But, Harte, did she love him?"

"Aye, she did, though it was hardship only he brought her, taking her to live apart from her own people. An exile that her own mother and daughter would also suffer."

Silence settles between them, and in the soft crackling of the flame and the moan of the wind, the child hears the beginning of the truth she has so long sought.

"Then that young woman was my mother."

"Aye."

"And the Northman, he was my father."

"A great sorrow to your grandmother that it should be so, for had her daughter married the son of the Chieftain the way she had arranged, her lot would have not have been to live out a lonely old age, an outcast on a distant hill."

"But she hated the Chieftain."

"That was only after the villagers had driven her to hatred with their scorn, and her only devotion became you and your mother."

"I can't remember how she looked, but sometimes I can hear her voice. I can hear her singing."

"She was a frail creature. Unlike your grandmother's

people in all but her auburn hair and flint-like anger that could spark and flare when struck with a hard word. And how they fought, she and your grandmother. Sometimes I thought she fell in love with the Northman to spite her."

"But my grandmother did love her."

"Sure, she loved her. That is just the way it is sometimes with mothers and daughters. But when you were born, being a widow herself, she chose to leave the village to live with her only daughter, weak as she was, and to help with the care of the baby."

"Me?"

The old man nods and smiles. "And a better world it is for your having been born into it, comfort that you are to me in my old age."

"What about my father?"

"You know now your father was that Northman, and that he chose for you an Icelandic name that means a battling swan, Svanhildur."

"Svanhildur," she rolls the sound so distantly familiar over her tongue.

"A swan for all its grace will battle to the death for its home. And that is the name you were given, child, a bird of beauty and a bird of war."

"But Mamó never calls me that."

The old man leans back and sets aside the branch he uses to stir the pot. "She cannot bring herself to call you by that name because to her ear his tongue is still harsh, and jagged are the memories of all the Northman stole."

"Tell me more."

"That, child, is as much of the story as I have to tell."

"But that's barely the beginning."

"The rest is for your grandmother to tell when and if she is ever ready."

"But what if she never tells me? I will never know who I am."

The hermit hesitates, and in that moment Svana senses his weakening will and knows that with one more wave of sympathy she can topple his resistance. "Harte," she pleads, "you know who you are. You tell me all the time about your heavenly father, and how it is his will that you live here on the beach apart from the others, and that gives you comfort. What comfort will there ever be for me if I can't know the same?"

Beaten, Harte shakes his head and sighs.

"Then go home and tell your grandmother, heavenly Father protect me, that Harte thinks it's time to tell."

"I will do that. I will."

The hermit turns away his head while she unwraps herself from the elk skin and pulls on her own wet clothes.

"Then leave me to my evening prayers, and be sure you will be in them, child."

Svana scrambles through the narrow gap at the base of the curving dry-stone wall and out onto the sand, hurrying back through the rushes to the cliff wall where she climbs the rocks to the grassy ledge, then up and over into the fields. Suddenly she stops. Crouching in the high grass like a small creature catching the scent of a predator, she clings close to the earth, peering out beyond the edge of the cliff where the moon casts a spear of light across the water. Minutes pass, but no one appears.

The ocean air smells of seaweed and the saltiness of a man. She crouches closer to the ground surrounded by the tall, dry grasses that shudder and sway, aware now of the throbbing pain that blurs her vision.

A mist settles on the field, and in her mind a memory unfurls of steam rising from a crusty loaf of bread that her grandmother sets down on the wide oaken boards of a short-legged table.

As if she is seated in the rafters of their hut looking down, Svana sees herself a toddler on tiptoe, the hem of her blue linen dress rising as she strains to reach for the *borreen-brack*, the sweet bread whose grainy smell intermingles with the salty night air.

In this vision appears the man who seldom came, whose eyes she always avoided, the one icy and blue crueler than the one glazed over in a milky haze. He enters the hut with a blast of cold air as gripped by hunger, the child throws her small body across the low table and rips off a chunk of the sweet loaf with both hands. She hears the thick laughter of the cruel eyed man when burning her small fingers, she howls.

Despite the searing pain and her grandmother's command to put down the hot bread, the little girl takes a bite in hope of finding the tiny coin baked into the bread for good luck on Samhain. When she feels the metallic weight on her tongue, she spits out the hot coin, smiling triumphantly at the thin bit of hammered silver that falls on the planks between them with a clink.

"Well done, lass!" her grandmother cheers with a grin that displays more gums than teeth.

When the little girl reaches with two hands for the clay cup of water, bringing it to her lips to cool her burnt mouth, down comes his thick hand to sweep away the silver coin that so briefly was her own.

"Stop to lick your burns and you lose the prize," he says

before rising and heading out still laughing, flipping the coin in the air with one hand and deftly catching it with the other.

That is all she can recall of the man who was her father. That and the image of the skin of his hands and forearms covered in rippling creases like the bottom of a dried-out streambed.

"Burns," was all her grandmother told her every time she had asked.

"Burns," she now repeats to herself, shaking herself from her sudden, dazed reverie. From where she still crouches hiding in the tall, buff colored grass, she sees the cowhide over the doorway of the cottage rise as if flung up by an unseen hand and feels a chill wind pass over her.

A bank of clouds passes over the moon, casting an eerie darkness over the hill. The shivering child springs to her feet and races past the rowan tree on the edge of the field. With its bare branches thrashing against the sky, it has shifted into a many-fingered beast about to pluck her up and toss her back onto the rocks below the ridge, to be hurled about once again by the frigid breakers.

The Silver Hand

Svana enters the dim hut where her grandmother still sleeps. Silently she slips off her mantle and spreads its dank folds over the low table by the fire. From a peg in the curved wicker wall she reaches for the nightdress that used to reach below her ankles but now barely brushes her knees. She welcomes the feel of the soft, dry cloth against her skin. Startled, she turns as a blast of wind pushes past the doorway, drumming the spotted cow skin with pellets of hail that fall onto the threshold and roll across the floor.

"It's wild night, a ghrá."

She crosses to the old woman and kneels by her side. "Mamó, you're awake."

"Surely, it's myself that does be wondering half the time if I'm opening my eyes on this world or the next, what with everything fluttering behind a misty haze that makes all hours night."

With a grunt she rolls onto her side, then bracing against her stiff and brittle arm, she slowly sits up and shimmies back to lean against the timber post. Sighing with exhaustion, she spreads the purple blanket across her lap. "Come sit by me, child."

Svana crawls under the thick weave of the coverlet and curls beside her grandmother who takes her icy fingers between her own weathered hands. "They're cold as cod still flapping in the net. Surely, you've been out walking the strand."

"But, Mamó."

"I'll not listen to you blather away as if Samhain were any other night of the year," she replies, her eyes bright with anger. "As if this night were not the wedge between two worlds, prying open the mouth of the hollow hills, the night when the spirits from the Other Side come spilling out all over Ireland. And there you are, strolling along the strand like it's nobody's business with any spiteful fairy beside you that happens to have a liking for the sea as well."

"But why should I fear the spirits when our own ancestors walk among them?"

"Aye, to be sure. But there are those who walk abroad on Samhain whose souls you'd not want for traveling companions."

"Like the Northman?"

Her grandmother's back stiffens, and her voice grows stern. "What do you know of him?"

Svana takes a breath before spitting out the seed of truth she has gleaned from the hermit's story. "I know that my mother saved his life and that he was my father."

Her rigid fingers clench the edge of the blanket.

"Tell me who's been filling your head with what's my own concern and no one else's?"

"It's my concern, too, and Harte says it's time to tell."

"The hermit," she utters with disgust. "He's spent so long conversing with the gulls, he's gone daft with thinking their squawking is the voice of some god from across the sea. It's nothing but foolishness he speaks."

"But I do believe him."

The old woman's breaths are more difficult, each inhalation a rumble and each exhalation a groan. Svana becomes silent, sorry for troubling her with hard thoughts, laying her cheek on her heaving chest. She considers her grandmother's eyes that even from behind the milky clouds that churn over them still flash with emotion.

"Not to worry, child. It would take all the ancient warriors in one phantom army to drag me to the Other Side. Not even *Tirnanóg*, that otherworld of peace and plenty, is a place I'd fancy going without you." She smooths the blanket over their laps, tucking in its folds around the child nestled beside her.

"I think Harte is right. It is time to tell."

"It's only time because you've both picked and poked until that wound is bleeding again."

"But I have to know who I am."

"Haven't I told you a hundred times? You are a true daughter Dé Dannan, the ancient people of the goddess *Danu*, the mother of all gods. It's the Dé Dannan who sailed to Ireland with their knowledge of all arts: music, magic and war. Your veins, a ghrá, flow with the blood that ran through the hearts of those warriors. What more is there to know?"

"I want to know about my father."

"And you'll not let me rest until you do."

"How can I rest with only half a heart in me?"

Her grandmother shakes her head, knowing that she is no match for the girl. "There are those who say the Northman was an outcast from his own land, and that even the briny ocean spat him out for the foulness of his deeds."

"But my mother pitied him."

"It was more than pity that shone in her eyes. For that

evening when she hadn't come home, I searched the strand and found her in the hermit's hut with the stranger's head in her lap, and on her face a look made me fear for her, for I knew by a glance that he was a Northman. But when I ordered her home, she refused."

"So, what did you do?"

"When the anger was on me, woe to any who stood between me and my will, so out I dragged her by the hair and led her kicking and shrieking back to the village. There I grabbed a stick of ash and with the gods as my witness, I beat her. But little did my anger do, for no sooner did I put that switch aside than she took off again."

"Did you follow her?"

"Only to the gate where she looked back at me with eyes that said our fate was sealed. I heard from the others that she nursed the Northman back to health. But when the morning came to gather on the beach where the Brehon was to speak a judgment, they were already gone."

"Where did they go? How did they live?"

"The Northman was no farmer. He hunted and he fished, and he knew like men of old how to clear a cave of wolves and make of it a snug place to pass a winter. But when she grew big in the belly, and her legs so swollen she could barely walk, he brought her back on a pallet dragged behind an ox. Near the spring that feeds our well he built her a leaning shelter, then set to work making this cottage of twigs and reeds and branches. After he finished the wattle frame, he daubed on the clay so thickly no chink would let in a ribbon of wind or a dribble of rain."

"Were you still angry?"

"By then my rage had been worn down by the worry that

knocked about in my heart. So when word reached me of their return, I took my loom on my back and left the village to live with her here and bring you into this world."

"Tell of the Northman, what was he like?"

"He was not a man to be easily known. He spoke little, but your mother being uncommonly bright learned his hard tongue during that year in the wild and taught him a fair bit of Irish herself."

"Did he care about me?"

"Had you been a son, perhaps he'd have taken more notice, but he was so little with us, never more than a few days at a time. So taut and restless a man I'd never seen before. Barely he'd sit himself down by the fire, but in the batting of an eye he'd be up and out in the open air again."

The old woman grimaces and her hands stiffen. Svana takes one and massages the fingers set in a rigid curve. In a few moments, the fingers flex and loosen.

"You've the healing hand," she says raising it to her lips.

"Mamó, how did we live in those days?"

"Much like now, with your mother to help me till the rocky soil and tend the garden. Ah, but surely the meat was more plentiful, for every time the Northman would return he'd bring enough badger and deer to smoke and keep us through the long months before he'd be back again. Once he brought with him a hefty ewe with three lambs and a little blue dress that he'd bartered in *Dubh Linn*."

"Were we happy?"

"It was a dark house when he was in it, but sure when he was away your mother would take to singing again. At milking-time she'd chant an air so sweetly, that it would soothe any restless beast, and whether it was spinning or churning or putting you down to sleep, she'd have a different song. At those times I'd say we were happy, but then that happiness was gone in a *bratha*, no more than the flit of a bumblebee's wing."

In the silence between them, the turf fire crackles. Svana watches the edge of a burning sod crumble to the ground and then, with a will of its own like a beetle inching away from the fire, it moves past the ring of white stones and crosses the earthen floor of the hut toward the doorway.

She blinks and tries to focus, but her vision blurs and the lump on her forehead pulses with a dull pain. Then from the bright ember a faint song emerges.

Listening, she thinks that only she can hear the song until the old woman heaves a sigh and begins to rock with its rhythm. Then with her eyes shut to this world, her grandmother sings the same sad ballad along with the voice that rises from the burning chunk of turf. And when their duet ends, the ember flares and a thin white flame shoots up before vanishing in a puff of smoke. With a groan, her grandmother shudders and her head droops toward her chest.

Svana springs up and shakes her shoulders. "Mamó. Mamó, wake up."

The old woman opens her rheumy eyes and stares past her toward the doorway.

"Sinéad?"

"Mamó, it's me."

"Aye, daughter, I see you there as surely as on that first morning of Beltene," she says, following a phantom to the fire with her eyes.

Svana sweeps the air with her hand, "Look, nothing. Nobody here."

"I remember how the air glistened, and you sat with the babe on your lap so that the new light of summer might fall on her and bring us good fortune." Her grandmother rocks, shaking her head. "But from that day on, only bad luck followed us."

Her eyes widen when a clatter of hooves approaches the hut then comes to a halt, and a man's voice falls like a fist on the wall of the hut.

"Pay!"

"I owe you nothing!" the old woman shouts back fiercely. "This hill was mine for the taking, so I took it, and it's not a thistle I'll pay you in rent. So be gone back to hell."

Svana stares at the portal where the cowhide moves like a tongue.

"Mark me, woman, I will be back for my money. You will pay." The horse whinnies before galloping down the hill.

"Bastard," she mutters, then turns again to the air beside her. "Remember how the next day at dawn he returned? But this time he was met with your husband's fist to his face!" For a moment her eyes light up triumphantly. "If only it had ended with that blow, but it was what followed that brought us to our lonely place on this hill. If only I had listened to you, Sinéad."

Again the old woman's head falls heavily toward her chest, but this time when she lifts it, her eyes search for the child, and she grips her hand firmly with both of her own, so not to be swept back into the spell.

"A ghrá?"

"Yes, Mamó, it's me. I'm here."

"Stay with me, child."

"Mamó? Was she here?"

"Surely her spirit does walk tonight."

"But why?"

"She wants me to follow."

"No, Mamó, no, you can't leave me, ever."

"No worries, girl, I'll always be by your side."

"And I'll never leave you alone again. No more walks, no more wandering. Just to the well and back. I'll go no further. I promise."

"There's an awful draft now. Do you feel it, child?"

Svana takes the purple blanket and wraps it around her grandmother's torso and hugs her tightly. "I'll never leave you like my mother did."

"I know now I was wrong. I should have listened when she said to go. When there was still time."

"Time to go where?"

"South she said. It had come to her in a dream that we should travel with her husband who was preparing for the season's hunt. But I couldn't leave."

"Why not?"

"For me it had been shame enough to be shunned by the village, but to be pushed from our home was more than my anger could bear. I told her to go if she wished, but I'd not let her take you, a tiny baby, traipsing the countryside. So we fought all day until the sun set, but the Northman had already left."

"Did my mother follow him?"

"She tried, but she couldn't track him and came back two days later, exhausted. It was on that day the Chieftain returned with his servant. Again I refused to go before the Brehon to settle our dispute, which was only a case of him trying to rob me. And so he knew how to get what he wanted by fasting."

"Fasting?"

"That's when a member of the tribe comes to sit outside the house of the one he claims has done him wrong."

"So?"

"So the whole time he's sitting there, it's not a morsel of food he'll take to his lips, and likewise the people of the house can eat nothing until they've paid the debt or made a pledge to settle the business before the judge. That Chieftain was no fool. He waited until your father had taken off again to the south to hunt and fish before he came with his servant who he left on our doorstep to try to starve us into submission."

"How long did he stay?

"For three days."

"I didn't eat for three whole days?"

"Sure, but your wailing would have killed us all. Your mother, weak as she was, couldn't nurse you with your appetite like a wild cub, so it was stir-about I fed you mostly, but what you favored most was *brechtan*, rich with eggs and honey."

The child licks her lips. "I can almost taste it still."

"Well you might, for it was the bowls of sweet custard that you howled for day and night, hungry little hound that you were."

"How long did you not eat?"

"Had it only been myself, I'd have fasted out of spite until the day the Chieftain's man fell over dead. But it was for your mother I feared, so after three days, I agreed to settle the claim before the Brehon just to get rid of that maggot."

"Did he leave?"

"Coward. When he saw no man about, he went behind the

house where we kept the livestock. But it was with me he had not thought to reckon."

"Did you thrash him, Mamó?"

"I took the meat fork from the cauldron and stalked him, and there in the yard I saw his thieving hand on the noose round the neck of my own best cow. So, with the aim of our ancestors, I hurled the fork, piercing his arm in two places, but he still made off with the ewe." The old woman pauses and breathes deeply before resuming her story.

"Hearing the ruckus, your mother dragged herself from her mat to the yard where she collapsed. I ran and lifted her from the puddle of blood that had formed beneath her and trailed behind us as I carried her inside."

"Why was she bleeding?"

"It's as if that fork cuts into my own flesh to recount those days."

"Then stop."

"Like water coming down a hillside there's no stopping it now, just as the day had come too soon for a second child to be born. He was a son, a babe no bigger than my open hand. And though I called upon *Dian Cécht*, the ancient healer of our people, before the sun gave out that day, they both had crossed to the Other Side."

"Did I cry?"

"For days there was no stopping the tears in this house, not yours or mine. Although being but a babe yourself, you could not have known the source of such grief."

Svana rests her head on her grandmother's lap. "I know now."

"There's only grief in knowing, child, which was why I fended off your questions until my strength to keep you from

BOOK ONE

the sadness was no match for your strength to know."

"Did he return?"

"Just after the feast of *Lugnasa* when the days were still long and hot. By that time he had enough of the Irish so that I could tell him about the fasting and how the ewe was taken, but when I did, the rage set on his face like mortar. That night smoke rose over the village, and the next day I learned that two houses, a barn and two stables had burned to the ground. They tracked him for five days, but there being no trace, they came back with talk of retribution against us. But the Brehon ruled that it could only be taken against the Northman, and they've left us alone ever since."

"Tonight I saw him."

"Who, child?"

"Him, the Northman. He had a cruel eye and a mean laugh, and he stole my silver coin."

"Whether it was memory or his own restless spirit crossing your path that was the look of him surely. Aye, he took the *pinginn* from you that night, and with the morning he was gone and never to return."

She nestles her head on her grandmother's lap. "So he didn't care about me."

"No more than a buck cares about last year's offspring. Some say he was slain in the south, some say he settled with his own kind in Dubh Linn and lives there still. But a curse on him in this world or the next for the misery he brought me."

Svana is quiet. In her mind she replays the story and feels her grief deepen as does her hatred for the Northman and shame for being his daughter.

"Hellish in life and dammed in death, may his Icelandic soul never seek you out."

The old woman untwines the girl's thick auburn braid while she sings a ballad about a glen and a young girl deceived, then reaches up behind her head for the small satin bag that hangs from the wall of woven twigs and polished hazel wood rods. With stiff fingers she tugs at its lace and takes out the white comb, carved from the antler of a deer.

"You've glorious hair," she says, smoothing out the tangles. "The same as was your mother's and mine. Same as all the women in our line flaunted, with its flecks of red to warn all who came too close of our willfulness and the blood of all enemies our warriors had spilled."

"Tell me again of our ancestors."

"Ours is a line that stretches back beyond the ancient time when *Cúchulainn* ruled Ulster and our own Queen Maeve ruled Connaught, Queen Maeve whose bones are said to be buried beneath the *mioscán* atop Knocknarea."

"The high hill beyond the field?"

"That very slope we used to climb where at its top there is the mound where we'd set down stones in her memory."

"Tell me again the part about the brooch."

She removes the silver sword-like pin that holds the heirloom to the tattered shawl wrapped around her sagging shoulders and hands it to her granddaughter.

"This brooch, a ghrá, is all that remains of those great days, so long ago they're nearly past remembering." Svana runs her thumb over the engraving, the crisscrossing swirls of wind and water, and the gap at its center like an empty well.

"Do you really think it held a gem?"

"Aye, surely. Back in those times gems were plentiful among our people."

She pictures summers past when her grandmother was out

working the soil with her *rán*, breaking up the clods and preparing the earth for planting. Then the silver brooch gleamed with such sharpness from her chest that she had thought it could blind an enemy. But the brooch has long since lost its luster, nearly black with years of smoke from the turf fire from which her grandmother seldom strays.

"Was it really forged by our ancestor?"

"How else would it still be in our keeping?"

"And what was his name?"

"He was *Goibniu*, and so powerful was his hand at the forge that kings wore his crested helmets, and the bracelets that encircled the arms of their wives came from his fire." Her bent fingers weave Svana's hair into swirling braids.

"And was it he who made the Silver Hand?"

"Wise it is to ask and ask again, so that the tatters of the old story are not blown off in time to be forgotten. Mend them, mend them in your mind."

"I will."

Her grandmother cranes her neck as if she sees the Silver Hand hovering above their heads. "The old stories tell us of a king whose hand was shorn off at the wrist in battle, and because no king with a severed limb could keep his throne, two kinsmen were called: Goibniu, master of the forge, and the other a physician schooled by druids in more ancient arts"

"And he gave the Silver Hand its power?"

"Aye, a ghrá, it was that magical thing that could drive the *Tuatha* to war or peace, a hand more fierce in battle and tender in love than any made by nature."

"Then if the Silver Hand was not of nature, was it a good or wicked thing?"

"In the old stories good and wicked twist like threads of

flax on a spindle. For just as the Silver Hand could be a thing of death or joy, some swore that Goibniu had learned his craft at the devil's own forge, but others that the lip of each goblet was trimmed with the light of dawn."

"I'd like to drink from one."

Her grandmother lowers herself wearily onto her bed of hides. "That, a ghrá, can never be, for all but this brooch has been lost to hard times and thieving hordes."

Over the doorway the leather flap flies upward with a snap. No one enters.

No gust of wind stirs the low and steady flames of the fire.

Then with a thrust, her grandmother sits up with a quickness long absent from her movement, and her voice rings out as strong and resonant as a harp. Her eyes focus on the doorway, and responding to an arrival that Svana cannot see, she calls out, "Welcome, you are welcome one and all!"

Motioning with her gnarled fingers, she directs the visitors to join her around the fire. "Gather round, my kinsmen, gather round."

"Mamó, don't," she warns, but her grandmother is attentive only to the newcomers as if Svana does not sit among them.

"Gather round," she commands, her words ringing out in silver tones, her eyes scanning the space around them. Then suddenly, though the turf fire still crackles, the temperature drops, and the hut feels colder than the ocean into which she plunged that night, and with the cold comes an eerie certainty that she sits among the dead. Her grandmother's head bobs and sways as her trance deepens. Then her voice rings out, "I'll tell it to you as it was told to me."

The child listens closely, her mind straining to take hold of this scrap of the old story, blown in on an unexpected gust of memory.

"So, it was no less than Lugh of the Long Arm, our most gifted warrior around whom the great men gathered, preparing for battle on the Plain of Tears. One by one he called their kinsmen forward to say what power each would wield in war, and so Goibniu was summoned."

To hear this new verse added to her family's history, Svana leans forward, but when her grandmother's voice drops into deep, guttural tones, she gasps. From her thin, chapped lips comes the voice of a man.

"Even if for seven years you men of Ireland battle, for every sword that shatters I will forge a weapon in its place more lethal. Mark me, no point will miss its mark, and no body pierced will taste of this life after."

She grabs the old woman's arm. "Mamó, wake up!"

Possessed, she turns her face to Svana, but her cloudy eyes look past her. Then whatever phantom has housed itself inside her body flicks its arm as if shaking off an insect, tossing her with a strength far greater than her grandmother's against the curved wall of woven branches.

"You all know my words to be no boast. I who forged the Silver Hand will make good on every claim. Now go with Lugh. Prepare to kill or be killed."

Again the flap over the portal snaps up, and the midnight void sucks the icy air from the hut and with it the phantoms depart, extinguishing the fire, casting Svana into an inky darkness. She tries to cry out. Her lips form words, but she can utter no sound. And like a fish plucked from the water flapping about on land, she struggles to breathe in the airless space. She scrambles on her hands and knees across the earthen floor to her grandmother's side.

With her mouth wide, her lungs clenching, she clings to the old woman who goes limp in her arms. But when a wave of salty sea air floods the hut, she swallows two breaths and her words sputter out.

"Mamó, don't go, stay with me."

With a moan the old woman stirs and the flame rekindles, the crackling sods giving warmth and the smell of earth.

"Are you alright, Mamó?"

"Tired, a ghrá, so tired."

Svana gently lowers her torso toward the ground and tucks the purple blanket around her, glancing warily around them. "Are they gone?"

"Who?"

"Them, the ones around the fire."

"No one comes here to our hut."

"But, Mamó, they were here and one spoke. Through you."

"Nonsense, child. If you heard a voice it was my own, muttering in my sleep. Just as you do each night. Now get me a drink, I've a terrible thirst."

Svana rises and crosses to the coiled clay pot on the table and dips in the wooden ladle. She scoops out the last sip which she tilts to her grandmother's parched lips.

The old woman barely sips before laying back her head and closing her eyes. She waits for her grandmother to stir and resume the tale, but when the bricks of turf turn to ash, disappointed, she bends to kiss the old one's brow. "Rest," she whispers and then reaching for the bucket by the door, sets off to draw water from the well.

Floating Bones

When Svana steps from the cottage, a burst of wind slaps her face. The damp leaves beneath her bare feet feel slick and cold as she steadies herself with an outstretched hand, half stepping, half slipping down the slope to the well. Gray stones border the gap in the earth wider than the length of the girl's arm. Kneeling beside it, she sees a bone white moon shivering up at her from the surface of the black water.

Her bucket sinks down with a splash when a shrill cry pierces the air. She freezes. Her eyes on the dark pool where the image of the moon resettles, she sees a rider on a broad-backed beast crossing the sky. Silently she crouches closer to the ground, a small tense animal alert to danger.

The sound of the cry again splits the night. She listens with terror as the howling rider descends, knowing that it can be no other than a *banshee*, one of the phantom women from the Other Side whose fearsome cry foretells death. Without raising her eyes, she watches the banshee yank hard on the reins, forcing its massive beast downward toward the edge of the field. Great tendrils of mist unfurl from its nostrils when with a grunt the wild boar hits the earth.

"You there, girl," the rider demands. "I have a task for you."

The rider dismounts and leads the boar by its curling tusk toward her. Svana shudders at the sound of the clattering bones that hang in a mantle over the wild boar's back. She dares not turn her gaze directly on the banshee, staring instead at its quivering image in the well, a square-jawed woman with cropped hair who wears leather breeches and whips the air with her riding crop.

"Scrub this beast. When I return if I like what I see, you will be rewarded. Do I make myself clear?"

She nods. Still looking downward, she hears the thumping of bare feet drumming the earth, then glancing up she sees the speeding banshee disappear into the air. The boar moves toward the girl.

It stands five times her width, its hide rough and caked with dried mud and its tusks cracked and yellow with age. But when the thick lids of its eyes lift and the beast's gaze meets hers, she sees nothing to fear, only dark pools of gentle weariness. She reaches up and strokes the beast that moves one step closer to her side.

"Poor beast," she coos and sets the filled bucket on the ground, steadying it with her hands while the huge animal drinks greedily, its thick tongue splashing the water back at her. When the boar finishes drinking, the girl steps to its side and straining upward with outstretched hands, she removes its coat of bones.

Reaching for a leafy branch from a nearby oak, she dips it into the well and begins to scrub the filth and grime gathered from countless night rides across the countryside and beyond. Svana dips and scrubs, dips and scrubs until the full moon of Samhain dangles on the bottom branch of a tree on the ridge of the hill. Like an over-ripe apple about to fall heavily from sight, it hangs and then drops just as the branch slips from her limp hand, and exhausted she falls by the great beast's side.

Then the thunder of a hundred hooves rolls over the hills, and a horde of marauding banshees touch down from the sky, led by two phantoms astride one boar. "Fine job, lass. And a fine reward will be yours after the hide of each beast has been scrubbed."

Their leader dismounts and tosses the armor of bones across the back of her beast. When she tugs at its reins, the great creature turns its sad, dark eyes toward the child. In the same moment all the banshees dismount and run after the rider, diminishing into the night, leaving behind the filthy herd.

The girl lifts the bones from each boar's back and scrubs, sometimes with vigor but sometimes with tenderness when her leafy branch touches a gouge or bloody bruise. While she works, the moon of Samhain, which has given way to an empty sky, reappears as a nut-colored sliver, and grows round again. Still she labors as days and nights tumble into untold time, and finally the herd stands clean and restless to resume their flight.

She falls at the base of the oak tree, her tired legs bent in the tangle of roots. Barely her head touches the ground when the sound of the banshees' cries again scare off her heavy sleep. "Well done," the familiar voice intones when at her feet she tosses an elk skin pouch.

"Banshees, ride," she commands her legion of riders who mount the snorting herd and then lift their voices in one terrifying shriek, rising to the sky as one trickle of light splashes across a gray and grimy dawn. She reaches for the pouch of rough hide and tugs at its lace. Rocks of gold and silver tumble across her palm. She returns them to the pouch, then rises and runs toward home, suddenly aware of how long she has been gone and how worried her grandmother must be.

When she pulls back the flap to the cottage, a hand grips her shoulder. "Svana, it's wrecked with grief I've been searching the hills to bring you back to your sick grandmother."

"Mamó?" she calls into the dim hut.

"It's not here that you'll find her."

"Then where is she, Harte?"

"She's on the other side of the hill, resting among those who journeyed before her."

Svana pushes past the hermit into the cottage and throws herself down onto her grandmother's bed of hides and her own purple blanket, realizing that the banshees' cry foretold her own grandmother's passing. Harte stands close by in the doorway, uttering prayers until she turns on him angrily. "Go away, leave me alone. What good is any god that takes without giving? Get out!"

"I'll leave now, but you know where to find me."

All through the day she huddles on her grandmother's bed until at twilight she runs from the hut and across the fields to the standing stones that mark the last place on earth where her ancestors rest. There a mound of loose earth blankets her grandmother's grave.

Hearing again the shrill noise of the banshees as their shadows flutter through the veil of clouds, she hurls the pouch of nuggets upward, tears of rage coursing down her cheeks.

Upward it rises beyond the force that holds her down, spilling its contents of gold and silver bits across the sky like shooting stars that sear the black night before exploding into a hundred thousand pinpoints of light.

Then she falls in a heap to the ground, surrendering to a heavy sleep. All through the raw and wintry night, she lies beneath the warring winds that bewitch her dreams.

Throughout the night the waves that crash below the ridge drown out a more distant tumult: the sounds of a battle etched on a wind that long ago swept over the field where ancient warriors clashed. Above the cries of men butchering and being butchered, there rises a fierce screech of carrion eaters. All through the night she struggles to awaken from the shadowy chaos beneath their vast wings.

At last when the wind retreats to wage its phantom war on the sodden memory of some other field, the night heaves a final moan, giving way to the silence of an ashen dawn. Awakened by its shifting light, the girl can barely raise her throbbing head from the ground.

When something rough and dry caresses her cheek, she lifts her eyelids that like every part of her body ache. There looking down with sad eyes stands the wild boar. The mist of each exhalation from its cavernous nostrils swirl downward, tossing about her tangled hair, encircling her body with the warmth of a living hide. The whirling mist of the wild boar's breath spreads over the hill, drying the dampness from the earth beneath her and dissolving the glistening dew. But this wind does not bow the tall grasses of the field, nor stir the brown leaves on the trees at its edge. It is then that the bones on the back of the boar begin to clatter.

One by one each bone rises, floating from the weave of the wild boar's armor. One by one each bone spins upward, and then inspirited they dance into a spiraling formation. Long bones, slender bones, thick and knobby bones they float and spin, keeping open a space at the center of their elegant vortex.

From their aerial company fly the disk-like bones that like tiny planets move across the inner space, aligning themselves in a curving slope to form the spine. Fascination struggling with fear, she watches them join together while the other bones bob and sway as if to the tune of some celestial piper.

How gracefully two arm bones bow to the shoulders, one whole and one shattered, swaying into place beside the ribs, which like open hands cradle the space that once housed a vanished heart. Finally the fragile bird-like bones fly down from their airy perches to nest in the grass, forming two feet that tap the earth eagerly. Then the remaining bones, so many and so fine, form the hands with outstretched fingers that reach for the empty space above its severed spine. The bent frame of a skeleton is complete, but headless.

She steps around the beast to make a barrier of its massive head between her and the bony phantom. When it raises a finger pointing eastward toward the crest of the hill and the boar follows behind its clattering gait, she turns and runs away.

Her heart pounds as she flees, stopping only when she feels her legs have gained a safe distance. But as she leans against the rowan tree, a force pulls her backward, dragging her through the wet grass until the claw like fingers of the phantom lock into her long braid and yank her to her feet, then lift and place her on the wild boar's back. Sickened by the touch of the bones on her skin, she shivers with revulsion. The skeleton then takes hold of the wild boar's reigns and leads them toward the hill.

It stops when they come to the well where two leaves land

on the water. Svana watches the crisscrossing rings and utters a prayer. Harte has taught her how to pray, but rather than chant the words to his god, she calls upon her grandmother to keep her safe. Warily she watches the skeleton's approach with its spine bent toward the earth. Then from the boar's neck it removes a long leather pouch before clattering toward the well where it kneels, pinching apart the leather lips, holding the narrow sack a hand's width above the water. Then from the well leaps a shining salmon, orange and pink, its taut body bright with strength and health. The skeleton then draws the lace tight, the fish still flapping within.

Her parched tongue rolls along the side of her mouth in search of a drop of moisture. When the skeleton clatters toward her, holding out the flip-flopping pouch, she takes it from the outstretched hand, careful not to touch the bony fingertips. The movement of the fish inside the pouch ceases. She holds the pouch and feels the liquid fullness of its contents as if the salmon has dissolved. Loosening the lace, she sips, but then drinks more greedily. Gulp after gulp the cool water slakes her thirst, and though she drinks and drinks, the leather folds of the pouch do not slacken. It is as full as when she began to drink.

She hangs the pouch about the boar's neck. Water spills out and splashes to the ground as the three resume walking. "At least," she whispers into the wild boar's ear, "whatever world we end up in, we won't go thirsty."

Moving toward the hut, they cross the plot of stony gray soil where each spring her grandmother has planted leeks, carrots and parsnips. Here the skeleton runs its rattling fingers over the ground until they start clawing the dirt like a dog. Svana fears that it is digging a tunnel to thrust her down into a world where banshees, phantoms and the headless dead do not simply visit on Samhain, but reside for all time. But then the skeleton stops. It grabs hold of a root and yanks until it falls backward with a clatter, clutching a huge turnip. When the skeleton falters to its feet and clatters toward the cottage, the boar follows, standing in the yard as the hide over the doorway flings up in welcome.

Setting down the massive root on the table, the skeleton sets to work sweeping out the ashes in the hearth and stacking the bricks of turf that she carried in on the eve of Samhain. As soon as it sets them down in the ring of stones, they redden and glow, sending up fiery tongues that lick the bottom of the black cauldron that hangs from a hook above the flames. Knowing fingers reach for the length of leather, rolled up and tied with a thong, where her grandmother always kept her thimble, needle and knife close at hand, and unwraps the utensils.

From the doorway Svana watches the skeleton hollow out the turnip and carve slits in its side. Next it reaches into the fire for a burning brick, breaking off a corner and tossing back the rest into the flames. When it places the small chunk, a red and glowing lump of ancient earth, inside the carved-out root, the lantern burns intensely, filling the hut with a fierce unnatural light.

Instantly the cottage heats up and the smell of grain rises from the cauldron. The headless one raises the pot from the iron hook and sets it down on the dirt floor, lifting its lid to release the aroma that makes her mouth water and her stomach contract.

Kneeling beside the cauldron, the skeleton pries up a crusty loaf with its bony fingertips and offers her the steaming loaf.

She grabs a hot fistful and even though it sears her fingertips, she hungrily bites into the grainy web of flour and air. Famished, she devours the bread from her burning hands until something sharp jabs her tongue. She spits out the chunk of bread, spattered with blood. Then in her hand she sees a glint of silver and rubs away the sand-colored crumbs.

It is her grandmother's brooch. The years of smoky residue that blackened its face gone, it now gleams, encouraging her with hope that the battered bones are inspirited by her grandmother.

"Mamó?"

But the bones give no answer, pointing instead to the purple blanket strewn across the bed of hides where her grandmother used to sleep. She stands perplexed until a thought as clear as any spoken words splashes across her mind like cold water over stone.

Bring it.

She retrieves the blanket, carrying it to the skeleton, draping it around the bones, careful not to touch them. Then in her hand she looks down at the brooch, the light from the turnip lantern bouncing off its silver facets. She unfastens the pin and reaches up to clasp the makeshift robe around the skeletal frame. The skeleton straightens its spine, rising to its full height, bringing its right hand to rest on the ancient brooch. Her heart races, for even without a skull, whoever's body these bones conveyed had stood two heads above her grandmother's height.

"Are you the Northman?"

A curt message comes disguised as her own thought.

No more.

The skeleton tucks the loaf under the long large bone of

what was once its upper arm. Reaching for the turnip lantern, it steps outside where a weave of white mist and drizzle refract the early morning light into a web of glinting hues.

Svana crosses to the doorway and looks out at the dazzling yard where the wild boar stands, twitching its ears and fidgeting beneath the enameled bridle and embroidered blanket across its back, red and edged with gold. Clearly the boar has been outfitted for a journey, and she has no doubt that she is the intended rider.

The skeleton gestures for her to mount, then stores the still-hot bread into the satchel strapped to the boar's side. Motionless she stands until the boar approaches and gently nuzzles her arm with its snout and then nudges her further into the yard where it lowers its back near a stump. With difficulty she climbs and seats herself sideways on its back, gripping the rein of the wild boar that lumbers across the yard. Turning to take one last glimpse of home, she sees the skeleton reach into the lantern, remove a red ember and toss it onto the roof.

"No!" she shrieks, watching the tongues of fire spread, lapping up the crackling thatch. Svana bows her twisted face into her hands, and remembering her father's seared and rippled skin, utters over and over, "Burner, Burner, Burner."

The skeleton clatters toward her and grabs hold of the wild boar's bridle and leads them down the hedge-lined path toward the sea.

Hill of the Moon

I hate you, I hate you: the words pulse through her body, reverberating on her skin as if it were the taut head of a *bodhrán*, the drum that urged the ancient warriors forward. He is her father, and she hates him, just as she hates whatever demon released him from hell to burn down her cottage. Rising from the pit within, her rage flares, searing her thoughts and blurring her vision. Through the slits beneath her swollen lids, she sees herself leap from the boar and beat the skeleton to the ground, scattering each bone as far as she can fling it. But her fear of the bones douses her rage, and her mind collapses into a heap of resignation that weighs down her heart under its white ashes.

Slowly they come to a calm and midmorning bright sea before shifting their direction southward along the shore. In the distance scuttling upon the rocks, Harte gathers seaweed into one basket and mussels into another. Sad beyond speech, the girl cannot call out the old man's name although she craves to hear her own voice and a human reply to know she has not crossed over to the Other Side.

Svana watches him approach, his old eyes angled toward the sand while behind him he drags the baskets, laden with his harvest from the sea. Surely, he will at any moment lift his head, and even though his eyes are glazed over with age, see her being borne off by the strange beast and the bones. And surely Harte will save her.

But when the old man is passing within arm's reach, all she can draw from her grief-stricken body is a nod. In return he responds with a vacant stare set on the dune behind the phantom travelers where his hut stands—a stare as vacant as the empty space her body has become.

She watches her friend rise over the dune, his baskets drawing two long ruts into the sand. After the hermit has disappeared without a parting glance or wave, she cranes her neck to see what she already knows. Neither do the footsteps of the bones nor the cloven hooves of the wild boar leave a nick in the dark wet sand. And although the sun is well up over the horizon, neither she, the boar nor the bones cast a shadow.

Now she knows her grandmother was right about the danger of the phantoms that walk among them on Samhain. How only the curving wall of their cottage had kept her safe, and how when she slipped on the hill toward the well that night, she had slid to the Other Side.

Turning up a path where a herd of cattle graze without raising an eye in their direction, the three pass the place where her grandmother always stopped to bow her head in respect for the ancient ones who rest beneath the tilting archway of stones.

Above the tomb a crow shakes out its wings and caws as they pass-by headed for *Knocknarea*, the place that Mamó used to call the Hill of the Moon. Crossing the field, Svana can see at its top the great stack of stones. According to legend, the mound has grown with the contribution of each visitor to the peak who sets down a rock in honor of *Maeve*, the warrior queen of Connaught. Ever since Svana could walk, she has climbed its gentle slope, racing ahead of her grandmother, holding up the folds of her mantle with one small hand as the other picked up stones from the grass, testing each for smoothness, before adding one to the mound in memory of the Queen said to be buried beneath it.

Svana now rises over the hillside on the back of the boar, her eyes on the flat-topped mound of stones where a crimson-cloaked figure sits. On none of her visits has she ever seen a pilgrim dare to set foot on the sacred mound, although more than once when her grandmother was not looking, she tried to scramble up. Drawing nearer to the crest of the hill, the skeleton stops and stoops down. Feeling along the ground, his bony hands raking and sifting through the grass and pebbles, he chooses two rocks.

When the skeleton clatters toward her and his fleshless fingers pry open her hand, the girl draws back. But when he gently drops one stone on her upturned palm and bows slightly, she feels a warm and sudden breeze and hears a word so often spoken by Harte: forgive.

"Never," she murmurs, throwing the stone aside as the bones lead the wild boar by its bridle up the final stretch of the climb. Svana dismounts at the top while the headless one sets down his stone at the foot of the cairn and then wanders off to sit on the eastern side of the hill.

She scans this ever-growing, grassless mound from which her grandmother always said the powerful Queen Maeve still kept watch over the Irish territory she long ago ruled. Svana observes the cloaked pilgrim. Wearing fitted trousers that end at the ankle with a strap that passes beneath sandal-shod feet, the stranger rises and descends the rocky slope. When a gust of wind throws back the hood of the brightly speckled cloak, it reveals a woman's face, framed with teaming masses of silver hair. She recognizes the features that she had first seen drawn on the sand and then swirling across the sky on the eve of Samhain.

"Welcome, cousin," she calls. "I am pleased you have arrived!"

"I'm not your cousin. My name is Svana, and I live with my grandmother. She is my only family."

"Believe me, child, there is no mistaking you. Truly you are my cousin, a daughter of Danu. And bequeathed to you is every fine thread of our story from the time the great elks first crossed the shallow water to this island and the nomads followed, through the arrival of our people and the wars of the ancient kings. For you are the living daughter Dé Dannan who will lead our tribe in battle back to its true destiny."

"I want to go home."

"What you want is of no interest to me." She casts a harsh look on the headless one who sits off to the side of the cairn. "First task done, you brought her. But don't think I am finished with you yet."

The bones skulk a little further off as Svana steps forward. "Who are you?"

"In life I was a fierce and lusty warrior at whose bidding battles raged, pulverizing the bones of my enemies into the soil. Men threw away their will to follow my desire. I was the Queen of Connaught, the greatest Queen of all Ireland."

"Queen Maeve, wife of *Aillil*?"

"Yes, I was wedded to Aillil, but in truth Aillil himself and all the court of Connaught knew him to be the husband of Maeve. In life I ruled all, including Aillil. But now in death I sit on this hill of stones, guardian of a barren coast. But a great battle will be fought, my warriors await my orders at *Tara* to rise up. Mark my words, daughter Dé Dannan, you have been led here by the Northman to help me conquer all Ireland."

"Why me?"

"Because you have the glints of copper in your hair that mark the women of our line, angry and willful, whose nature will take you over the bridge of time from the land of the living back to the shores of Lough Arrow where our warriors still battle. You will retrieve the Silver Hand of King *Nuada*, the same that led the Tuatha from the day our ships landed. With my fingers wrapped around its wrist, I will raise it in battle and conquer all the tribes of Ireland. All Chieftains will pay tribute to Connaught, so that there will be no doubt who is the richest ruler of all Ireland."

Dashing up the rocky slope, an avalanche of smooth stones rolling down beneath her feet, Svana shouts, "If you want the Silver Hand, go get it yourself. Leave me alone! Just because you're a queen doesn't mean you can tell me what to do!"

"Enough! You will do as you are told."

"This isn't fair. I'm going home!"

"What you call home is no more than a heap of ashes. But *Ushnaugh* can be the palace where you reside for all time, sleeping on sheets of satin, dining at boards heavy with fresh roasted game and grilled salmon, tasty cakes and trifles."

"The only home I want is with my grandmother."

"Ah, but she is dead, and now you are an orphan. But be the daughter of Queen Maeve, and you will share the riches of our warriors' victories."

"I hate war."

"Then you know nothing of the clash of swords and the cries of your enemies vanquished and the rush of power when you've beaten them back into the earth."

"I only know what I heard that night I slept on my grandmother's grave."

"One must not be weakened by the pathetic cries of the defeated, but hardened by them. That is the mark of a leader of men."

"My friend Harte says that there is one ruler more powerful than all others, a god who sent his son to earth to speak of love."

"Harte? The monk who huddles in his hut over there?" she laughs pointing toward the shore. "What can a monk know of love?"

"He told me the son of that great god is the Prince of Peace and that his mother is a peasant girl, and that one day she will return at the end of time to squash the head of the serpent that poisons the world with greed."

"If she lands on this shore I'll kill her with my bare hands, because without war life is worthless, for the only life worth living is lived at the expense of your enemies."

"The only life I want is my own."

"It appears that what you called your life, no longer has any worth at all."

With clenched fists, the girl charges. With her chin tucked down, she rams with her head and rapidly punches. The Queen does not flinch, but in one motion grabs her wrist and spins around the flailing girl, twisting her arm sharply behind her back.

"Let go," she shouts, struggling, grimacing with the tightening of Maeve's grip.

"Listen to me, daughter of the despised, stop being a peasant brat and I will not only release you, but send you on the journey of a lifetime."

"Let me go!"

"Bring me the Silver Hand and we will wage war against the Irish usurpers. Make me the only Queen of Ireland and you will be my daughter for all time."

"I won't help you make your stupid war."

"Then I will tend to the wars and you can tend to the pockets of peace in between. There's profit to be had in both."

With the shadow cast by a cloud crossing overhead, Svana feels her life on the hillside slipping further away. She has to act, and even if it takes a wicked alliance, she has to get back home.

"Then I can have whatever I want?"

"When you bring me the Silver Hand, whatever you desire," Maeve promises, loosening her grip.

"Anything?"

"Anything. Just bring it to me."

"Then tell me where to find it."

"Good choice," says Maeve releasing her. "I have dragged this miscreant from hell to guide you through the shrouds of time to Lough Arrow. From there you will seek the Silver Hand that will lead you to Tara where I will meet you at your journey's end."

"But what if the bones get lost?"

"Then you will both be doomed to wander, a phantom child and her father among the shades."

The thought of losing all hope of home is more than the she can bear. Her hazel eyes become two quivering pools that flood over her cheeks, and in those tears Queen Maeve sees the chance to win over her weakening will and beckons to where she sits in the cool grass.

"Come to me," she coos. Exhausted, Svana obeys and sits beside the Queen who takes her hand. "You must understand that we are family. We share the same blood and that makes us both daughters Dé Dannan." Gently she pulls the weary child closer and rests her head on her lap, smoothing back the tangled hair and healing the swollen welt on her brow with her fingertips. "Together, child, our gifts will burn brighter than the stars that are crowning Knocknarea this windy night."

"I just want to go back before Samhain."

"That life will dim in the shadow of Ushnaugh. But for now rest," she murmurs, "just rest."

Queen Maeve's voice bewitches her with a song that lulls her to sleep. And even the wild boar after having been ridden hard by banshees for centuries without rest, sleeps through that windy night. Not until a vein of pink runs across the sky, does Maeve move from her, setting down her head on a mossy mound and approaching the place where the skeleton cowers.

"You, Icelandic burner, did you not think that from this height I could see your shore and the captives that you herded like cattle into a shed, the Irish women your half-brother claimed as his—the dispute you settled by tossing a red-hot coal on the thatch of the stable where they slept with their own babes? Did you not think that I could hear the screams that rose on fiery tongues that night? Burner, it was you who could not read the symbols that unfurled in black smoke above your head, spelling out your doom!"

The thunder of Maeve's voice rolls down the hillside. Her fury awakens Svana who stirs and listens while the bones quake and clatter.

"Burner, vengeance like a knife left in its sheath does not go dull. My time came to drive that blade into your fate, and it was my rage that wracked your boat and sank your cargo, and it was your brains I meant to dash against the rocks.

But because you had no fear, you stayed to deceive a young girl on my own shore, my own kinswoman. You wooed her with your Icelandic eyes, my cousin who died laboring to bring your bastard son into this world."

She then turns to the girl. "Svana, know the story of the Burner and his foul deeds for which he has so far tasted one full decade of his doom. He is your father, the unrepentant burner for whom there lies one chance in you to be reprieved from an eternity of that hell."

Then Maeve hurls the skeleton against the mound of stones, scattering the bones at her feet. Trembling they come together again, and though she knows she hates him even more for the history that she has heard, the Northman's daughter feels a shard of pity.

"Know, Burner, I have summoned your bones to lead this daughter Dé Dannan in the quest for the Silver Hand. Bring it to me or be damned. Both of you. Now go."

With those words the once great Queen vanishes, and Svana hurries to join the clattering bones that have run ahead of the wild boar, hastily making its retreat down the eastern slope in the direction of Lough Arrow.

Skull

A mist has settled over the mountain. As the three descend, it rolls down the slope and spreads over the surrounding fields of Sligo. Beneath its veil, Svana's sadness deepens. Its folds thicken, masking her from the countryside and driving her into the whorl of her own dark thoughts with only the slit of light from the turnip lantern carried by the bones to cut a path through the haze.

Days pass into weeks and still the fog does not lift. Although in her depression she feels neither thirst nor hunger, she forces herself to eat the bread, still warm from the leather satchel slung over the boar, and drink the water still fresh from her own well that splashes about in the sack that never empties. When the headless one stops by a high bush bright with tiny red berries, she reaches out to pluck a handful of the gleaming beads of fruit. She knows them to be the same tart berries that at the end of summer her grandmother used to boil down into a tonic to ward off sickness. Then as they walk, she chews the rose hips one by one, knowing that although she has crossed the pale into this netherworld, she might not be beyond disease.

Each night when they stop, her father gathers the kindling to make a fire and construct his daughter's bed of brushwood, moss and rushes. Shaky with exhaustion, she dismounts and, takes the thick blanket from the boar's back still warm with the animal's heat. She wraps herself and lies back on her rustic bed while the bones sit fitfully by her side, waiting for dawn so he can rise to fetch her breakfast from the saddlebag and wake her, anxious to resume their walking.

And so each morning she must again climb on the back of the patient boar, submitting to the monotony of the ride and dull torment of her own thoughts. Her grandmother gone there is nothing remaining of their life but a heap of ash and charred branches, nothing except the silver brooch that clasps the purple blanket around the battered bones, rattling by her side.

One night when they camp by a brook, she watches the skeleton walk down the bank into the churning water and stand motionless by a ledge of flat gray rocks. With a splash a shimmering trout emerges from the water, flapping between the skeleton's bony talons. Soon the sizzling of its skin and the smell of its flesh grilling over the flames pique the girl's appetite, and for the first time since their journey began, she devours her meal hungrily.

Full and vaguely content, she lies back on the mat of ferns and moss spread over a framework of oak twigs and searches the pinpoints of light above for familiar objects that remind her of home: a ladle, a pot, their deer antler comb. Then in the night sky appears the head of her grandmother's cow blinking back at her.

Soon she is asleep, but instead of her usual nightmares, she dreams of a meadow in summer, studded with small blue flowers. From the shadowy woods and through the tall grasses a man and child emerge. Svana recognizes herself wearing the blue linen dress that falls to her ankles, its tiny pleats flowing with each step—the dress her father brought from Dubh Linn with the white embroidery bordering its hem. On it she wears two brooches, identical to her grandmother's but for the red and blue gems that gleam in each.

The man by her side is the Northman. He wears leather armor beneath a thick gray cloak, and above his shoulders floats an empty iron helmet. They cross the field to a path along a ridge overlooking the sea. Looking down, she sees the village children circling her younger self, curled up and silent as the others hurl sand and shells and stones at her huddled body.

Svana grips her father's hand more tightly as from his hut the hermit emerges who, having heard the game shift to warfare, comes running down the beach, flailing his arms and yelling for them to stop. The children disband with wild yelps and cries, running back toward the village. Then the old man kneels beside the broken child who curls up and sobs, "I am not the burner, I'm not."

When she awakes, she understands the taunts and feels the full weight of being the Northman's daughter. Over and over these thoughts play out in her mind as they journey toward Lough Arrow. Green fields and stony fences, standing stones and more green fields. She comes to know the vastness of an acre when the heart is weighed down with despair. Still the mist does not lift.

Led by the bones, the wild boar lumbers southward with the listless girl swaying in the saddle until abruptly one morning the beast halts. Startled, she looks out beyond her own misery to see the shore of a placid lake. Beneath the churning fog Lough Arrow ripples blue like the hem of the dress in her dream. She dismounts and kneels on the bank to admire the sapphire water that eddies and swirls, tracing the movement of a breeze that rises and sweeps the shore, dissolving the mist and the damp chill that had clamped her heart.

Around the rim of the lake, the fields take on a new luster while along the bank sails a swan and its mate—their white forms like pearl bright moons in a morning sky. Svana feels her depression lift. Stepping into the water, she draws up her slip and mantle, her bare feet sinking in the mud. For a moment she stands entranced by the tiny translucent fish that swim in circles around her ankles.

Alert to her reawakening senses, she is unaware that the bones have waded out into the lake. With increasing distress they fall below the surface of the water, the skeletal hand raking the ground, roiling up the mud. Flailing in frustration, the bones let out a moan that makes the leaves of the overhanging tree tremble.

Startled, she trips backward, scattering the minnows as her heel hits something sharp and begins to throb. Beneath the churning mud and rising mist of her own blood, she sees what seems to be a broken bowl. When she reaches down for the object, her own thoughts are overtaken by the phantom.

This is the place.

With urgency the skeleton grips her arm, the tips of its bones like the talons of a predator piercing her skin.

Give it to me. It's mine.

The voice cries out as her fingers grab the object. Drawing it from the water, she cups the form in her hands and sees that it is no broken piece of pottery, but a cracked and yellow skull. The skeleton's agitation grows. Waist high in the water that streams through its frame, it struggles, reaching for the skull which its daughter holds beyond its reach. When she draws her arms behind her back, the headless one lunges from side to side, trying to grab the skull.

"Burner! Why should I give you anything when it's only shame you've given me?"

The skeleton turns away, teetering in the water that laps the shore. "Tell me. Did you die here?"

The skeleton braces itself against a rock. No reply crosses her mind. "Fine, don't answer, and I'll fling it out so far into the lake it will remain a house for fish forever!"

His voice again streams across her mind.

Don't! I'll tell. I was killed by my half-brother who tried to steal my slaves from me.

"Your slaves? Women and children torn from their own homes. Slaves? You deserve to go back to hell for what you made them suffer."

The skeleton bows its shoulders.

Those fires do await me.

"How did you die here?"

Fog rolled over the lake where I bathed. I was a naked man without a blade to meet the blow that lopped off my head. So I died without honor, without kinsmen or cremation to free my soul from these decrepit bones.

"Honor? You speak of honor? You who dragged women and children away to claim them like cattle. What pity should I have when in life you cared for no one?"

The skeleton leans on a rock.

In my life I cared for one.

"Liar!"

I loved her.

The words sail across her mind.

"Liar," she shouts again, crossing to the rock where he sits, the skull trailing in the water behind her.

I loved Sinéad.

Infuriated by the demon's mention of her mother's name, Svana draws back, ready to attack the bones with its own skull. But as lake water streams from its brow, there in the sockets, she sees two tranquil pools where swim two tiny silver fish. She is careful not to displace the finned creatures that swim in circles—so fragile and beautiful that she stops, for a moment mesmerized by their watery movement.

Forgive.

The soft plea laps along the edges of her mind.

Forgive.

The word comes again, washing over her mind. "Then say you're sorry."

Standing above the bones that have fallen in the currents of the lake, the Northman's daughter holds the skull in her hands like an old Irish crown above its headless frame.

There by the shore of Lough Arrow the headless skeleton bows before the girl who raises the skull and sets it back on the spine from which it was so long ago severed.

I am.

Like the water lapping the shore, the words wash across her mind, dissolving the icy fringe of her hatred. Extending her hand, Svana helps the bones of her father stand.

"Then in my mother's name I forgive you."

The skull nods slightly as the tiny fish splash from one socket across what once had been the bridge of his nose and into the other small cavern that had held his useless eye.

Side by side they stand on the shore of Lough Arrow beneath the white birds that circle overhead. Watching them dip and sail on the warm breeze that blows off the last tendrils of mist from the lake, she recalls Harte's story about the peasant girl chosen by heaven to give birth to a prince who at the end of time will crush the serpent's head with her bare foot so that peace will fill the world.

She remembers that she asked the monk how she would know the girl had come, and he replied by pointing to the sky on that cloudless morning. "Her robe will be that shade of blue. And its hem will flutter across your heart."

Standing there beside her father, she knows by the color of Lough Arrow that the peasant girl must dwell nearby, waiting for the end of time because here in this peaceful place her torment has left her. Then like a sign from Harte's heaven, white flakes fall to join the water of Lough Arrow. Tilting back his brow, the skeleton stands still as the snow glistens white against his ecru bones while Svana marvels at the flakes, too beautiful to last more than a moment on the coarse fabric of her mantle.

Hags of Kesh Corran

The folds of mist that had briefly parted soon close back over the lake, its islands and surrounding mountains. Beating the ground restlessly, the wild boar snorts and turns from the shore as pellets of hail the size of coarse salt pit the surface of the water. Rapidly they fall, bowing the dry, buff grasses that fringe the bank, tip-tapping softly, urging them to move on.

Tilting up his skull, her father's bones rise and cross to Svana. This time she does not draw back when he touches her arm with the tips of his fingers.

Whatever we face, I'll protect you.

The bones then take the reins of the wild boar and lead the beast beside a granite boulder so that his daughter can mount. But when she grabs hold of the bridle, pressing down on the rock with the tanned leather sole of her shoe, a low, gravelly voice rises from underfoot.

"Daughter of the Tuatha Dé Dannan, descend…"

First she leaps down, but then steps back onto the rock that drones, "Daughter of the Tuatha Dé Dannan, descendant of Goibniu."

"The stone knows who I am!" she says, jumping down and beckoning her father who moves slowly toward her. "Go on, step up. You've nothing more to hide, have you?" Warily he sets his foot against the stone.

"Son of…" He pulls his foot away, the silver fish leaping

with agitation from one eye socket into the other.

My name will only cast its shadow over you.

"Stand on the stone."

With his skull sagging toward his chest, he steps up on the blue-gray stone

"Son of the tyrant *Turgeis*."

The name sets her mind into turmoil. Turgeis—plunderer, murderer, burner. Even living alone on the hill, Svana had heard from Harte of the Danish invader whose brutal scourge ended with a stone about his neck when he was drowned by an Irish king.

Turgeis—feared, hated, reviled. Turgeis, father of her father. Sensing his daughter's revulsion, the skeleton draws away as the hailstones fall more heavily.

What in life was my pride, in death is my shame.

She crosses to his side and rests her hand on the brooch. "I gave this to you, and now I give you the name of him who forged it and those who have kept it safe. You are one of us, the Tuatha Dé Dannan." The skeleton rests his bony fingers across her hand, and for the first time Svana smiles at him.

Even thicker the pearl gray haze hangs down, grazing the shore of Lough Arrow where the icy pellets litter the bank like the periwinkles she used to gather on the strand. Then her father's words cross her mind.

I know a place, a cave I found for your mother on our way to the south.

The pellets of ice bouncing off her cloak, she rides the wild boar following the strand of light from her father's lantern through the thickening storm. They come to a path that leads across a bog where she can barely see the timbers and rough planks beneath her feet. The walkway sinks deeper into the soggy ground with each step of the boar. Many miles they walk, the hailstones ricocheting off their backs to the brown green earth. Then they come to the foot of a hill. Her father points upward.

Kesh Corran.

Svana peeks up from below her mantle at a cave with two portals that seem to stare back down with the eyes of a warrior from beneath a helmet. She dismounts, and they begin the ascent. Stumbling over the loose stones and icy pebbles they approach the cave. Her father is struggling beside her, clawing at roots with the wind whistling through his bones when a hoary missile knocks the lantern from his other hand. Its stripe of light spins from hillside to blackened sky, from hillside to blackened sky as the carved turnip rolls down the steep, rocky slope. She feels a pang at the loss of the lantern, but the raging winds beat her attention back to their inch by inch ascent.

Finally they rise to the portals of *Kesh Corran*, but just as Svana dives into one of its ashen eyes, down crashes a hailstone the size of a crab, knocking her father's skull over the ledge. His agonized moan fills her mind, driving her back into the fists of the storm. The icy wind snaps at the folds of her cloak and fills the fabric like a sail. She can see the skull dangling from a gnarled root, and kneeling she leans way over the ledge with outstretched fingers, the pebbles and stones of ice beating down on her back. With her other hand, she grabs hold of a branch that snaps as she falls forward, knocking the skull onto a flat rock just beyond her reach.

Shrill laughter rings out from the mouth of the cave. "Its lid, the demon's lost its bloody lid." A high-pitched shriek joins the howl of the wind to create an eerie chorus.

Svana angles the branch downward, skewering the skull with the forked tip into the sockets. Tossing aside the stick, she peers inside to where its two inhabitants stare back at her, calmly fluttering their fins. Clutching the skull to her chest, she plunges back into the dark chamber where the fits of insane laughter still echo, the old woman gagging on her own saliva. Bracing her heaving body against a rock, she watches the girl hurry toward the bones.

"Its lid, she's gone and got the bloody lid." Her laughter subsides into a snicker as she watches her set the skull atop the shuddering bones. "Now why do y'want t'go n'waste a thing like that on them useless bones. Surely a skull the size of the demons would make a fine goblet for me ale."

"He's not a demon!"

"It's a demon all right. I knows 'em when I sees 'em, and that one there's a bad 'un."

Svana squints into the passage. Her eyes adjusting to the darkness, she makes out three grotesque forms. One, a heap of human wreckage on the ground, its mangled arms and legs, jutting out at disjointed angles as if they'd been broken and reset by a maniacal physician. The others, a pair of hags equally decrepit with age, are connected by a length of thread that runs from the distaff held by one and the spindle by the other. Matted clumps of orange-red hair crown their balding scalps.

"Needn't be afraid of us, girleen. Come closer. Let us have a look at you."

The two busy themselves with their work as the girl inches forward. The flax that is wound loosely around a rock is held by the one who flaunts her green gums in a grotesque smile, feeding the thread gradually with her withered left hand to the spinning-stick that her partner turns, twisting the material into thread.

"A girleen, a demon and a beastie, strange bedfellows y'be. But surely we be glad t'have ye, ain't we, Skein?"

"A hundred thousand welcomes to Kesh Corran," the other hag chimes in, jutting out her bearded chin, smiling to show off the stump of a single gray tooth that hangs from her sagging gums. "A hundred thousand welcomes."

"Who are you?" Svana asks, leaping back when a crab-like hand from the human mound on the floor of the cave scratches her ankle.

"Just as y'sees us. Three poor old sisters as keeps bodies and souls together the long, cold winter here at the head of Kesh Corran. I be Camog, this be Skein an' the ugly un's the oldest, Holly."

"A hundred thousand welcomes," twitters Skein. "A hundred thousand welcomes."

"Shut yer gob!" Camog barks. She then turns a pitiful look toward the girl, her voice softening into a sickly sweet trickle. "What with the one gone in the head, and the other gone in the legs, it's a hardship for sure that it's me has t'care for 'em. Why the old one there can't so much as crawl from the mouth of the cave, can ye, Holly?"

The twisted one cowers and rocks.

"Y'see what burden I be bearin', left here on Kesh Corran to care for the old un's meself."

"I see," says Svana and, despite the revulsion that would have sent her scrambling back down the hillside if fists of hail were not still crashing down, she does feel pity for these old people.

"Seein' as the storm's been kind enough to bring ye to Kesh

Corran, the least we can do is make the girleen a mug a tae," says Camog, rising to her bulbous feet. "While I go n'gather some kindling, would ye draw n'twist the threads for Skein?"

"I don't know how," she lies.

"Well, then I'll give the spinning over to the bones."

"A hundred thousand thank yous," twitters Skein.

"Ah, shut up," Camog snaps, passing the distaff to the skeleton. "Y'don't mind, do y'demon?"

"I told you. He's not a demon."

"Surely," Camog chuckles. "An' just as surely as the bones be no demon, it's I who'll be the wife of Lugh of the Long Arm. Handsome 'un as he is."

"In yer dreams," cackles Skein with a spray of spit.

"In me dreams, indeed. In me dreams not fit for tellin' t'such fine company as be comin' t'visit. Come now, Sir Bones. Will ye sit a wee bit closer t'me sister as I think she fancies ye?"

"Look, Camog, a little fishy!" squeals Skein, squinting into the eye socket of the Northman's skull. "Better, sister, better still! There be two!"

"T'is foul winds that bring no good fortune, and it's kippers we'll be havin' with our tae!" Camog rocks with laughter at the skeleton that leaps up, the fish in his eye socket withdrawing back into the skull.

"Sit ye down, Sir Bones, we just be playin' with ye a bit. Sit ye down!" Svana looks to the portal of the cave where the hailstones still come crashing down. There Camog stands in the thin light, gray as gruel, looking out wistfully. "Dreams not fit for tellin'," she warbles to herself. "Dreams a me the wife a Lugh. So handsome as he be, we'd make a right good match."

"Surely Lugh be han'some," Skein chortles while her crooked fingers spin. "Too han'some fer the likes a ye."

Camog lunges back across the cave at Skein, her twisted fingers bent into a vice around her sister's scrawny neck. "So ye think it's funny, the likes a me an' Lugh together?"

"No," she gasps. "I just was thinkin' on his good looks is all."

"Thinkin' that the likes a me might never get more from him than a wad a spit on me bunions, that's what you be thinkin', ain't ye?" Skein cowers as Camog hovers menacingly above her. "Ne're would the likes a him so much as curse an old hag the likes a me. Is that what y'be thinkin' too, Sir Bones?"

"Father, run now!" Svana yells, yanking on the bridle of the wild boar which instead of responding to the tug of her hand, falls in a heap on the floor of the cave.

Camog releases her cowering sister and crosses the cave toward the girl.

"T'is unkind of ye, girleen, t'take the beastie without it takin' its rest."

"You did this to him!" she shrieks, still tugging at its reign.

"Young folk's today be so rude, so rude, ain't they, Sir Bones," laments Camog. "Skein, will y'look n'see what Sir Bones is gone n'done to hisself, all wrapped up he is."

"All wrapped up," echoes Skein.

"'N'such a mess he's gone n'made a yer spinnin'."

Svana runs to where he sits bound, the flax from the stone distaff having wound its way from bone to bone, binding shin to femur and arms to ribs. She tears at the threads with fingers and teeth, but cannot break them.

Run.

"I won't leave you."

Moving closer, Camog studies the swirls of the silver brooch that clasps the homespun blanket around his torso. "An' what's this, Sir Bones?"

"Skein, look at the pretty bauble the demon does be wearin' on hisself. A thing like that must once belonged to the likes of a king, wouldn't y'say so, Skein?"

"A king surely," parrots Skein.

"Camog's old enough t'know a thing a value when she sees it." The hag turns to Svana. "So, y'three be tomb robbers, eh?"

When Camog's gnawed and filthy fingertips tap the ancient heirloom, Svana springs across the cave and strikes back her gnarled hand. "That brooch was worn by one in life who was greater than any king."

"Now calm yerself, it's just a poor old woman I am, and I mean ye no disrespect. But who might such a one a'been?"

"She was the mother of my mother, a daughter Dé Dannan."

"A daughter Dé Dannan, d'ye hear that Skein? Well, daughter of a daughter Dé Dannan, what brings y'then to our humble hill?"

"We're just travelers passing, and it's only the storm that drove us inside this cave."

"An' t'where might y'travelers be headed?"

"We've been sent to Lough Arrow by Queen Maeve to find the Silver Hand, and so you must release us as we're on the Queen's business."

"Oh, Maeve, now she be one we know well, eh, Skein? A right old friend, Maeve."

"A right old friend, Maeve, a right old friend indeed."

"Why she n'Skein likes the same things: blood'n battle, eh,

Skein?"

Skein rocks and giggles, "Blood'n battle, battle n'blood."

"Me sister likes it best when they send in the boys."

"Battle, blood n'boys. Battle, blood, n'boys. I likes 'em young the best!" she squeals with more delight.

"More than one time Maeve's been kind t'us, n'more than once I threw a battle her way. Sure, but Maeve's a right old friend, and if ye three be friends of Maeve, ye be friends of ours."

"Battle, blood n'boys."

"Shut up now, Skein, or it's yer own blood you'll be tastin' when I rap yer last twisted tooth out'a yer gob."

Skein whimpers and slinks further back into the cave.

"Then let us go."

"Now, now, ye rest a bit while meself n'Skein go n'gather kindling to make a wee fire before ye three be goin' on yer way. Ye'd not deny n'old woman the pleasure of a mug a tae with her betters, now would ye? Come, Skein," she commands, stepping from the portal of Kesh Corran with Skein scurrying close behind like a small dog.

Svana reaches for a shard of stone to cut at the threads that bind her father. But as desperately as her fingers work, she can neither cut nor undo the twists and knots of flax which in her efforts to unravel them, wind round and round her wrists and up her arms until bound to her torso, she cannot move them.

Late afternoon dims into a dull evening, and the silence of the cave is disturbed only by the occasional whimper of the crippled sister and the rustling of a thousand wings as bats fly in and out of Kesh Corran, the stench of their droppings fouling the cave.

"C'mon, c'mon!"

Excitedly Camog urges someone up the hill. In the threshold of light cast by a full moon, the hags appear, breathless and beckoning to one behind them.

"You'll be thankin' me surely when y'sees 'em. C'mon."

A voice, clear and strong, rings through the cave. "I know your tricks, Camog, and if you're lying, my blade will speak my thanks."

"Go on n'look f'yerself. It's the silver brooch of Nuada hisself, g'on n'look. They been to the tomb, I tell y'true, Lugh. They been to the tomb. And she says they're going back for the Silver Hand."

From where Svana lies looking up into the corridor of moonlight, a warrior appears illuminated around the edges. Beneath his sleeveless cloak she admires the satin folds of his mantle, deep blue bordered by a crimson stripe, and the elegance of his yellow hair that softly frames his bearded face beneath its hood. Around his neck the young man wears the twisted strands of a silver and gold torque, and hammered bracelets ring his thick and downy forearms.

Ready for battle, he holds in his left hand the leather strap of a circular bronze shield that has been burnished bright, its concentric circles gleaming in the moonlight like the surface of a pond. From the belt that crosses his waist hangs a slingshot, and the hilt of the sword protrudes from an enameled scabbard. Although he stands barely a head above the shrunken witches, his muscular form conveys power.

When he approaches and the folds of his cloak part, Svana sees with astonishment that the silver brooch fastened to his mantle is the same as her own, but for a blood red stone set at its center.

"Y'see, y'see, Lugh." Her claw of a hand is beckoning him closer. "Look at the demon's chest. It's there, Lugh, same as yours and your kinsman, king before ye, Nuada, the very one he wore when he fell just the other side a Lough Arrow. The one ye buried him with. The one he stole."

Lugh kneels beside the skeleton, examining the brooch.

"It is," he says, tipping his sword beneath the brooch and with a quick slit plucking it up from the blanket and catching it in his left hand. "Except the thief pried off the stone."

"Sold it already, have ye? Ah, the shame of it, stealin' from a dead man, a king no less," Camog prattles. "Y'see, Lugh, I told ye they was tomb robbers. Now run 'em through an' toss 'em on the bog. Toss 'em out all three!"

"Shut it, hag."

"But I thought ye'd thank me, Lugh. I thought ye'd be pleased n'thank an old woman for her kindness," whimpers Camog.

"She thought maybe you'd kiss her," hisses Skein grinning grotesquely.

"Shut up!" shrieks Camog, striking out with her cracked and dirty nails to claw her sister's face that shrivels into a whimpering mass of wrinkles.

"She drew blood, she drew blood, she did!"

"I'll not say it again, hags!" Lugh draws the blade of his sword ringing from its sheath. "Another word and yours will be the first two carcasses on the bog."

Then a guttural cry rings through the cave, and the third sister drags her lame body across the cave floor on her elbows. Her face twisted in pain, she throws herself across Svana's bound body.

"De... de... de," the sister stutters.

"Just run 'em both through, Lugh, only do Holly first, the useless cur," screeches Camog.

"De... Dé Dannan!" She spits out the words, her body convulsing and her head jerking with the grotesque effort of her speech. "Dé Dannan," she sputters again, striking the chest of the stunned girl beneath her.

Lugh bends over them, his sword poised, ready to respond to any falsehood. "How did you come to possess this brooch, demon?"

"He is no demon, he is my father, and I am a daughter Dé Dannan."

"Hideous liars!" hisses Camog. "Don't you believe 'em, Lugh, for they robbed the tomb surely, and it's back they'll be goin' t'steal the Silver Hand for the fine fortune it'll bring to a couple shabby thieves the likes a these."

"Silence, hag," commands Lugh in a voice that would have cut short any other than the witch, her face mottled with rage, the blood vessels writhing as if about to burst and spout, yellow spittle foaming from her chalky lips.

"Kill 'em I say, murder, murder, cut'em down afore they've a chance t'steal again!"

Delighting in the blood that any moment might be shed, Skein squeals in demonic chorus, "Murder, murder, cut'em down, Lugh, cut'em down!"

His mouth clenches and a muscle twitches below his eye when raising his sword in one sweeping arc, he lops off the two heads that fall with one thud to the ground. Above the dry skinned skulls, the withered bodies teeter before toppling to the dirt where from their bloodless trunks, slither out two halves of a white serpent. Meeting in the dirt, they fuse into one and rise, striking out with a hiss at the bound girl. Its gray tongue is taut until Lugh's sword strikes again, severing the serpent which drops like two pieces of rope to the ground. From the limp halves now slide a hundred milk-white worms that slither into the dirt, sinking down into the earth below Kesh Corran.

With the grip of Camog's spell broken, the binding threads unravel from Svana and the bones, as the wild boar stirs and rises shakily on its legs. And where Holly's shattered body had lain, there now awakes a bewildered young woman.

"Let's leave this den," says Lugh, turning toward Svana. "If you spoke the truth, then we three are cousins, and you've nothing to fear. But if you've invoked the name of the Dé Dannan falsely, then your end will be as quick as theirs."

Holding tightly the reins of the boar, Svana follows, breathing in the cold sweet draughts of night air, leaving the stench of the witches' cave behind them. But still she fears the anger of this warrior if he learns her father's true origin. Lugh leads the way out onto the hillside where wisps of clouds speed across the sky. To Holly who falters, limping beside him, he offers his arm.

"Thank you. I've long been the captive of those two hags whose unnatural life they sucked from me. With the return of each winter my body became more crippled, so that they could survive another year."

"Long have your fair seasons been missed, and happy will *Dagda* be at your return." With the wind at their backs, they make their way down the hillside toward the lake.

Cauldron of Undry

With the gaping mouths of Kesh Corran behind them, Svana rides the boar along the bank of Lough Arrow, following her father, Lugh and the witch who hobbles by his side. Steadily they move toward the fire that blazes near the place of the name-speaking boulder from which they departed the previous morning. From the flames rise a plume of smoke and flying cinders that sweep upward in the breeze as a wide shadow bends over a cauldron. Then from this gargantuan form comes a belch that bellows down the bank.

"Dagda!" calls out Lugh. "Too much porridge again, eh, lad?"

"Never too much, always enough and then maybe a tad more for good measure!"

Dagda wears a brown homespun tunic and short hooded cloak and rubs a thick hand over his stomach, nearly as wide as the cauldron that burbles and spits over the fire. Encircling the approaching party, the aroma, a mixture of meat, leeks and wild mushrooms, speeds up their pace and makes Svana's mouth water.

Behind the wavering of light and shadow cast by the flames, she studies Dagda's face. His green eyes flicker and dim, surrounded by creases that have been formed by centuries of laughter, each crease smiling when the great one chuckles. In the moonlight his long matted hair, white as the caps of waves, is dashed about by the breeze that blows off the lake. Stirring the contents of the pot with a branch of an oak, he picks at the bits of his supper from the beard that rolls down the hill of his chest in two curling streams. "I see you brought guests to taste the hospitality of Undry."

"That depends on what says the stone."

"Come now, Lugh, even enemies have eaten from this pot. And even if it were their last meal, no men but cowards have ever left its side unsatisfied," declares Dagda whose name Svana knows means the good god, and whose *Cauldron of Undry* has provided food and wisdom through the ages.

"Well, at least I'll know whether I dine with friend or foe, honesty or lies. You, girl, step up on the stone."

She comes forward, unafraid for herself, but worried of its outcome for her father, the Icelandic Invader, son of the tyrant Turgeis.

"Daughter," the rock intones, "of the Tuatha Dé Dannan, descendant of Goibniu."

Dagda bellows with laughter and crosses over to the girl who he lifts far above the rock in his bear-like embrace. "A mere slip of a thing, but she's one of our own!"

"You there, bones. Step up."

Svana holds her breath while the skeleton clatters forward and raises a foot above the granite surface. "Go on if you've nothing to hide. Otherwise, let's have an end to this farce." She moves closer to her father and steadies him with her hand so he can balance his foot on the stone.

"Son of the ty... son of...."

"I've never know the stone to falter," says Dagda in amazement.

"Step up with two feet then," orders Lugh, growing

impatient with the stuttering stone. The girl helps her father up onto the rock, knowing whatever the outcome for him will be the fate she will choose for herself.

"Father of Svana, descendant of the Tuatha Dé Dannan."

"And who the devil is Svana?"

"I am, and he is my father," she replies, relieved that her father has been rescued from the shadow of the deeds of his father, the tyrant Turgeis.

"Welcome, Svana and Father Bones," booms Dagda, hitting the skeleton with such good-natured force that he knocks out five vertebrae which topple down through his rib cage, clattering onto the ground at their feet, causing another wave of laughter from the giant. Svana scurries to retrieve them and set them back in place.

"It's not funny."

"If not for the laughter, I'd not have lived half this long."

"And half as long would have been twice enough for ten times ten mortals," chimes in the witches' captive who has been hovering on the edge of these proceedings. She hobbles over to the campfire, smiling at Dagda.

"Why, Lugh, it's Holly! Come closer, lassie, and don't hide from your old friend any longer. We've not seen you for a decade, and brutal the seasons have grown without your hand to hold back the rain or soften the wind."

"Camog and Skein had cursed me into a silent, twisted thing up in Kesh Corran," she says, her voice muffled by his beard as he hugs her tightly.

"Dagda, the girl didn't survive the witches' depravity to be smothered by a daft old bear."

"If it's daft I am, Lugh, it's not with the years that are on me, but the pleasure of the fair wind that has brought friends and family together this night." He settles his thick, furry arm around Holly's shoulder. "And what of those hags?"

"They slithered off as hideous white worms that were kinder to the eye than their former selves."

"Aye, that's welcome news, for the world's a more beautiful place without their twisted faces to behold. Why the memory alone is nearly enough to put off my appetite," he says with a shudder. "But not quite. Come gather around, kinsmen, and enjoy the abundance of Undry!"

Dagda crosses to the bubbling cauldron that hangs suspended from the iron hooks planted on each side of the fire. Formed of gleaming facets of bronze, his cauldron is no mere pot. Great craftsmanship has gone into its making and its conical rivets have been precisely welded into place, its cavern deep enough to stew an entire cow for a battalion of guests.

"Always enough, never too much and maybe a tad more for good measure." He jabs a meat fork into the stew and comes up with a joint of ox. With a flick of his wrist the steaming bone slides off the double prongs and onto a wooden plate that Dagda hands to Lugh.

"And what's your pleasure, lassie? Lamb or boar?" At the sound of these words the wild boar snorts and stamps the ground. "Sorry, friend," says Dagda, then turning to Holly he adds, "we've only lamb left."

"Thank you, Dagda, but tonight I'll dine on fresh air and the sweet smell of new grass."

"And I'll join you," says Lugh.

Arm in arm the two move toward the bank where he removes his cloak and spreads it over a mossy patch for Holly to sit beside him. Steadying herself on his arm, she lowers herself onto the shore.

"Is she a witch, too?" Svana asks Dagda.

"Aye, but a good one whose soft nature can soothe the most savage storm. You'll not see the like of yesterday's hail stones now she's back. And what of you, lass? Are you still mortal enough to eat a hearty meal?"

She nods eagerly, the aroma rising from Undry having given her a sharp hunger. Sitting beside her father by the fire, she happily accepts the oaken bowl of steaming stew that Dagda sets on her lap. She dips in her wooden spoon and brings a tender white chunk to her lips. Firm yet soft it melts into the gravy in her mouth.

"Delicious, but that bite wasn't lamb or *mecon*, nothing that grew in Mamó's garden."

"That, my child, is a taste of Ireland's future. That's potato."

"Potato?"

"Sure, you've never tasted it before. It will be a few generations before it is planted in Irish soil." She takes another bite, savoring the taste of leeks and lamb, blending with the buttery morsels of potato. "Hearty enough to thrive in our rocky soil, plentiful enough to feed a small family of twelve."

Having hidden since their encounter with the witches of Kesh Corran, the tiny silver fish swim to the portal of their caves and peek out, creating their own currents with their ceaselessly wavering bodies.

"Why there's two wee fish in your head, Father Bones!"
Tenants from Lough Arrow.

"He says, they're tenants from Lough Arrow."

"Aye, there comes a time when all mortals are but landlords to tiny creatures."

I'd rather house the fish than worms. In life I favored the sea.

"My father says..."

"I can hear the Northman, girl."

"So, you've known all along?"

"Icelandic invader, son of Turgeis. All newcomers to this island are known to the Dagda. But not to worry, Father Bones. Your daughter has made an Irishman out of you."

It's only from this side that I can see my own misdeeds.

"Sure, but it's not the Northmen alone who plunder and burn. Like ourselves you love the clash of your swords and your own battle cries as much as you love your own laws and your *míd*. It's the race of men that's beyond their own nature I'm waiting to see, the race that savors the pleasure of the winds of peace more than the bloody rush of battle."

Svana holds out her bowl for more stew. "So why don't you put aside your weapons?"

"A simple question, not so simply answered." Dagda, dips the ladle into the steaming pot. "I'm a warrior, and where the Silver Hand of King Nuada leads, I must follow. It's the wisdom or the folly of our leaders that drives us beyond the dictates of our will. It's madness surely, but so it stands. Right, Father Bones?"

The skeleton nods, the minnows splashing out one socket and into the other. Suddenly his daughter springs to her feet, startled by the bush beside her that rustles and shakes with snorts and grunts.

"Easy, lass, that's just Bridey's swine rooting around for her supper. Here, girl," he calls to her as he sets another steaming bowl on the ground.

Snuffling the ground noisily, the pig hurries over to the campfire, her massive pink body moving almost daintily on her cloven hooves toward her supper. But catching a glimpse of the wild boar, she stops, turning up her snout in the air. "No lady, no matter how fine, has ever turned up her nose at a meal from Undry. Now eat that or there won't be another serving, you fancy gilt!"

But the pig will not eat. Instead she nudges the bowl in the direction of the wild boar, and raising her eyes to meet his gaze, she tilts her pointy ears and softly grunts her invitation. "Well, go on, lad," he urges the silent beast who seems equally taken aback at these feminine advances. "Surely, you'll not be turning down so beguiling a creature?"

The wild boar, despite all his fearless adventures flown across the centuries in service to the banshees, shyly nudges the bowl toward Bridey's swine.

"Eat!" thunders Dagda. Then bowing their heads together, the two begin to guzzle down their meal, slopping the stew over the lip of the bowl, then lapping up the puddles of meat and gravy from the matted grass.

"Now that's more like it!" Dagda approves while Svana laughs at the sight of her companion in love. "You see, the belly of Undry holds more than meat and potatoes. In that cauldron's all you'll ever need in a lifetime. What is it you need, lass?" he asks plucking a wide, dry leaf from a stem of a branch and handing it to her.

"I need to know where we're going," she replies, wiping the traces of gravy from her chin.

"Before you figure that out, you need to know where you've been. And I'm guessing you've barely a clue, now have you?"

"I come from the hut above the hermit's cloghan on the strand."

"Sure, many the times I've joined you by that fire to hear you defend the honor of the gods. But before that?"

"Before that I wasn't born."

"Well, if you've not learned that being born's not the only way of being in this world, then you've not learned much. Why Lugh and I've been born and died a hundred times and still we're roving the countryside. And what of Maeve scuttling up and down the rocks of Knocknarea. With only the gulls to command, and still as haughty and demanding as ever."

"I didn't want to come here, she made me."

"Typical of Maeve, not many have ever said no to her," laughs Dagda. "She thinks herself charming, but she's about as beguiling as a bull. Not even poor Aillil who married her for the sake of Connaught, the only province without a king, but after a few years of the wrangling that went on in that marriage bed, he had only himself to blame."

"She wants the Silver Hand so she can rule all of Ireland."

"Bad enough she's driven Aillil into the ground, but with the Silver Hand she'd be the end of us all. For if that warmongering whore could, she'd draft us into her private wars for all time. Don't tell Lugh I told you so, but between you and me, I'm weary of the wars."

"Not Queen Maeve, she wants to fight forever."

"To hell with Maeve, what is it that you want? The Cauldron of Undry is as bountiful with stories as stew."

"Tell me more of my ancestors."

"Let's start with Lugh, who by birth is not a son of the Tuatha, but rather our ancient enemy the Fomorians."

"Not of the Tuatha?"

"Long before his birth, there'd been a prophecy made by

their druids who told Balor the King he'd be slain by his own grandson. His wife wailed, indeed all the ladies did, but he had his own daughter locked away in a crystal tower on Tory Island so that she could never bear a child."

"Was she lonely?"

"Desperately, but our healer, Dian Cecht, soon heard of her loveliness and found his way to the island and up into the tower. So deep was their love that he stayed with her, bringing her food and caring for her in her distress. And so with the passage of that year, the daughter of Balor gave birth to three hearty sons. Enraged, her father sent a handmaiden to wrap the babies in a blanket and toss them over the edge of the whirlpool. Now whether it was by luck or mercy, one babe slipped from the folds of that cloth and under a hedge near the swirling waters that drowned his baby brothers."

"How terrible."

"Aye, it was awful."

"What of the one under the bush?"

"It was your ancestor, Goibniu, who chanced to hear him wailing. Lifting up the tiny naked babe, he brought him back to his own hut and raised him as his son."

"But what of Balor? Did he not try to kill him again?

"As far as he knew, all the brothers were dead, with only the god of the sea, to father them."

"And what of the prophecy?"

"Prophecies are not so easily undone. By Goibniu's forge, the child grew to be a warrior who so surpassed all others in the arts of war and peace, that King Nuada of the Silver Hand saw in him a strong ally."

"The night before my grandmother died, she told of the battle on the Plain of Tears," Svana says, recalling the phantom conference around their turf fire.

"I know, lass. I was there!"

"She said that it was around Lugh the warriors gathered."

"Indeed, it was Lugh who King Nuada trusted above all others, and rightly so, for only he could deliver us from bondage. So all agreed in council that Lugh should lead us in the war."

"Did we win?" she asks scraping the bottom of her wooden bowl.

"Thanks only to Lugh—for we were on the edge of defeat when he noticed that the one eye of their leader, his own grandfather the ogre Balor, had begun to twitch. You must remember that his eye was a noxious thing, and to look on it in battle was death surely."

"How can an eye be deadly?"

"Long before the Fomorian druids had been brewing an evil potion. Being a curious lad, Balor had come and looked into the pot, but when the fumes of the concoction settled on his face—one eye was wiped away like a shell on the sand washed away by a wave. The other eye was poisoned with venom so potent that when the eye opened, it would kill any who looked on it. Which was why even as a king, he was forced to live in darkness as his eyelid could only be raised in battle."

"Maybe that was why he was so mean."

"It's your own kind nature that does say so, but with or without an eye, Balor was wicked through and through."

"So what happened?"

"We were just on the edge of losing when Balor summoned his servants to prop up his eye. Lugh heard the order and took the sling shot from his belt and a stone from the hollow in his shield where he kept his ammunition. Just as they pried up his eyelid, he took aim and he let fly his *tathlum*."

"What's a tathlum?"

"A missile made by druids of the blood of toads, bears, vipers and sea sand. And lucky for us all, Lugh hurled it across the battlefield with such force that it drove Balor's eye out the other side of his head, slaying twenty-seven of his own warriors and causing the rest to scatter in terror."

A gust of cold wind sets the flames leaping over the crackling branches. As Svana's teeth chatter, her father takes the purple blanket from his own frame and wraps it around her.

"I heard that battle on the hillside the night I slept on my grandmother's grave."

"A bloody battle to be sure, where men and boys fought toe to toe, inflicting such agony that the sound of it still passes down to each generation of the Tuatha."

"I hope never to hear that hateful noise again."

"Nor I, but not until the voice of the many drowns out the voice of the few, will the brutality end."

Svana yawns, her eyelids drooping as her father rises to make her a bed of branches, moss and dry grass.

"But, Dagda, when will that be?"

"That is for the gods to decree."

"But my friend Harte says that there is only one god's will that drives the world."

"Well, be it many or be it one, when finally we're ready to give up the battles in our own minds, Tirnanóg will be the place where we all can take our rest."

But the sleeping girl does not hear him, for the bones of her father have lifted her from the ground and set her down slumbering on the soft, dry bed he has made not far from the fire where he sits down beside her.

A voice cuts through the silence that has settled on the campsite. "Here pig, pig, pig," cries a woman coming out of the woods. She is tall and broad-shouldered, a handsome woman whose braids hang down to her waist, but her face is pinched with anger. She crosses to Undry and sniffs the rising fumes. "Dagda, I swear by Danu, if my pig is in that porridge, so help you."

"Hold your tongue, daughter, before you go making any oaths you'll be sorry to keep. Besides, she's not in the pot."

"Who's the stranger?"

"That's Father Bones, a renegade from *Valhalla*, come to join our ranks by his daughter's side."

"Welcome. You haven't happened to see a sow running about, have you?"

"Is it not a hundred times I've told you, *Brigid*, you can't keep a wild pig for a pet. They've a life of their own to follow."

"A life that too often ends in Undry."

"Is it so little faith that you have in your own father?"

"Well, then if she's not in the pot, Dagda, just tell me where is she?"

"She ate from Undry not an hour ago, and then took off with a suitor."

"A suitor? But she's never shown interest in any such nonsense. After all, she's still a baby, she's just a gilt."

"Bridey, just because you've turned away more men then there are grains of barley in the fields of Ireland, doesn't mean she has no use for them."

Bridey scans the shore. "Which way did they go?"

"Off into the woods."

"Well, if she heads back this way, send her home. Good night, cousin," she says with a wave toward the skeleton who raises a bony hand in farewell.

Branches crackle beneath her sandal-shod feet as Bridey strides away from the campsite where loud snores rise from Dagda whose head nests in his matted beard. While she is sleeping, Svana's father gently combs out the twigs and bits of broken leaves from her hair, separating the glossy strands with his bony fingers and crisscrossing her long red tresses into intricate braids.

Crossing Lough Arrow

"Will you look at her, a right little Northman princess," chortles Dagda, standing above the sleeping girl who stirs at the sound of his laughter.

Svana half opens her eyes and then shuts them again against the glare of the midday sun. "Dagda, what are you going on about?"

"Hasn't your father made a Viking lass of you with those two braids wound around your ears like two lazy snakes in the sun? I wonder would he be willing to do mine up the same," he adds, tossing his disheveled locks over the cliff of his shoulder.

"Oh, Dagda, you are daft."

"Daft or no, at least I've the decency to get up before the sun is staring me full in the face. Now up with you. Undry may have the patience to simmer for ages, but I'll not stand here stirring the porridge all day."

Facing the cloudless sky, Svana sits up and shades her eyes. Tossing off the heavy folds of the purple blanket, she realizes that in the hours since they descended Kesh Corran, the seasons have shifted from winter to mid-summer, bypassing a wet Irish spring. Having slept so many nights on a makeshift bed inches above the damp earth and waking each morning under a blanket of dew, she arises this morning for the first time without the stiff ache in her muscles or chill in her bones.

Instead, setting her bare feet on the ground, she feels the silky warmth of the grass on the soles of her feet and inhales the fragrance of the wildflowers that burst in a frenzy of blossoms along the edge of the lake where Lugh approaches with Holly. A ring of tiny blue trumpet-like flowers encircles the silver tresses that fall past her narrow waist. "So, are you hungry for some breakfast, lassie?"

"I'll not say no to the hospitality of Undry."

"That's all I ever hope to hear from any man, woman or child who comes to sit by her side. It's them that say, no thank you, I've just eaten, or I'm getting a bit round about the waist that make me want to put the meat fork through their gristly hearts."

"You'll not hear that from me, Uncle."

"Sure, not with your appetite like a newborn cub." Dagda ladles the oats speckled with plump bits of currants and apple into her bowl. "Too bad, Father Bones, you've no stomach left for the food. Life in any realm without a rib or a pint to wash it down would indeed be hell."

The skeleton nods in agreement as his new family gathers round the morning fire.

"And what was your destination, cousins, before you were bushwhacked by Camog and Skein?" asks Lugh.

"Our destination's not our own. It's Maeve who has sent us to Lough Arrow."

"Had you told me in Kesh Corran that Maeve sent you, I would have run my blade through you as surely as I cut down those hags."

"Wherever it is we're going, I'm glad our journey led us here where in one night I learned more of my past than in all my years."

"Do you hear that Lugh, all her years? And how many of those have there been?"

"How many I can't tell, but Mamó said that I was born on the first day of *Errach*."

"Well, if it's not on my own daughter Bridey's feast day you were born, the day when first the sheep milk flows with the promise of a mild spring."

Svana scrapes the porridge from the bottom of her bowl and licks her spoon.

"Have you had your fill, lassie?"

"I have surely." She hands him her spotless bowl wiped clean of every grain. "But maybe just a bit more."

"That's the way it always is with Undry. Never too much, always enough and a tad more for good measure."

"Thank you, Uncle, for the porridge and the stories."

"No need to thank me, lassie, the story's your own."

"And, surely," adds Lugh, "the story is as much your birth right as the silver brooch. And now that I have no doubt that you are its rightful inheritors, let me give it back to you."

From beneath his mantle, Lugh removes the brooch that he had taken in the cave and pins it to the purple blanket that hangs loosely about the frame of the seated skeleton. But instead of being blackened with smoke and age, the brooch gleams with a metallic luster that heightens the beauty of the gem at it center.

"The stone's back, but, Lugh, it's not red like yours. It's blue! The same color as Lough Arrow the morning we arrived. Look how it shifts and shimmers like the water."

"It's an omen, that's certain. But what does it mean?"

The stone bodes peace.

"Surely that would put the likes of us out of business, eh,

Lugh?"

"War is one business I'm ready to be rid of. And if that's the purpose of your journey, then let's be on our way."

"Lugh you're the last warrior I'd have thought would ever talk of retirement."

"Dagda, if there's better things to do, I'm ready to hang up my shield on the wall of Tara forever."

Holly, who has been sitting cat-like on a boulder in the sun, rises and stretches. Walking toward the gathering around Undry, she reaches behind her ear for a sprig of waxy green leaves and tiny berries, and then crossing to Svana, she weaves its slender branch into her braided hair.

"May this sprig give you hope till your journey's end, and may we all be there to welcome you home."

"Now that will be a gathering to end all gatherings," chuckles Dagda.

The same healing herb clings to the hardwood in the North.

"Some call it Golden Bough, others All Heal, but it is the sacred clinging plant. Five days after the new moon of the long night of winter, we harvest it from the oak tree with a golden sickle. The sprigs must be caught before they touch the ground to keep its healing power."

In the North when enemies meet by chance beneath it, they must lay down their arms and honor a day's truce.

"Yes, peace is the Golden Bough's most potent gift, but only those warriors powerful enough to lay down arms can enjoy the healing power of its oils." Svana wraps her arms around Holly's waist. "And without you coming to Kesh Corran, I would have rotted away in that dank, dark cave."

"And a waste to the world that would have been, not to know your goodness. Or yours," says the girl, taking hold of one of Dagda's rough skinned fingers in her small hand.

Dagda bends down to hug her then stands up, blinking and brushing away the droplets that glisten on his beard. "Damn, but it's the warm months of *Samhradh* that always burn my eyes and make me sniffle like a boy hanging on to his mammy's mantle."

A small boat carved out from the trunk of a pine tree bobs and sways on the edge of the lake behind a cluster of bushes. When Lugh crosses toward it, two swans emerge, one raising its chest like a shield and thrashing the water with its wings. As he unknots the rope that moors the boat to a root that curls from beneath the bank, Dagda laughs from shore.

"He's ready to battle you for the lake, Lugh. Better push off."

The angry male lunges toward Lugh, its feet beating the water as its mate swims out from its nest behind the bushes. When Lugh raises the oar, the male retreats, turning to swim behind the female as she crosses the lake, followed by two young cygnets.

Svana scans the shore for her companion the wild boar. But it is not her sad-eyed, lumbering friend that approaches. For scampering toward the camp fire he comes, transformed by the presence of Bridey's swine who trots by his side.

"I'm not sure he'll be bearing you any further, lass."

Crossing to her friend who looks away guiltily at her approach, she strokes his great snout and bristly hide. "You stay here. I wouldn't want you to sink our boat halfway cross Lough Arrow." She removes his saddle bags, bridle, and the cloth *dillat* that softened the many miles of her ride to Lough Arrow. The boar bows its head and gives the girl a nudge before grunting his farewell and prancing off merrily with his fair lady by his side.

By the shore Lugh steadies the canoe for the skeleton who steps into the hollow trunk. "Come, cousin, we must be off,"

The girl runs to Dagda who sits by the fire and stretches her arms as far as they can reach around his mountainous shoulder, nestling her head against his matted hair that smells of wood smoke, new grass and roasting lamb. "I'll miss you most of all."

"And I you, lassie."

Dagda places the saddlebag of endless bread and the pouch of endless water over her shoulder. "Don't forget these. I know what a powerful appetite you have."

"Any more blather and it'll be the end of a fortnight before we set off," shouts Lugh. "Hurry up!"

"I'll miss you," Svana calls out over her shoulder as she runs toward the boat. Lugh dips the carved branches into the water. With each pull of his arms, the boat moves across the lake while on the shore their friends shrink in the distance.

They have nearly reached the middle of the lake when there is a blinding flash. In her mind Svana hears her father groan as the minnows leap from his skull, doubling and tripling in size with each slap of their tails on the bottom of the boat. She catches one between two hands, but it wriggles from her grasp before both fling themselves in a glistening arc back into the water.

When her father's spine straightens, he raises his head, and there in the caverns where the fish had been, there are two eyes, one blue and the other hazel.

The world's a dazzling place.

"Did things not appear the same in life?" asks Lugh.

Nothing like this.

"So, has death enhanced your vision, Father Bones?"

Far beyond imagination.

Her father stares out at the lake in quiet amazement.

"I've not seen the like as wondrous since the Silver Hand turned into flesh."

"But how did it come to life?"

"Though Goibniu forged it and the tribe's physician attached it, it was still a useless thing. It only came alive when the physician's son, Miach, chanted the magical words: Joint to joint and sinew to sinew, joint to joint and sinew to sinew."

"Joint to joint and sinew to sinew." Svana chants along as below the dark surface of the water, a snake slithers near the boat.

Listening to the splash of the oars in the water, she watches clouds gather, followed by a flash of lightning that cuts through them, piercing the lake. She waits to hear the crash of thunder, but there is no sound as she notices the gleam of the snake swerving into a pattern.

"Look there, Lugh!" Svana points to where the slithering body of the snake has drawn the form of the Silver Hand pointing eastward.

"It points toward Tara."

The snake submerges while a gust of wind pushes the curragh from behind, hastening its progress toward the shore from which rises the clash and cries of battle. Lugh rows steadily without speaking while the sun moves swiftly westward. Darkness overtakes the lake as iron black clouds roll over the sky.

"Please, Lugh, let's row back to Holly and Dagda," Svana begs, but Lugh does not answer. He has fallen deeper into a trance, scanning the fast approaching shore. Over their heads dips and caws a hooded crow, its feathers white and edged in black that form a cowl over its head, its wings vast and its cry incessant, seeming to urge them forward.

"*Morrigan*, I can row no faster."

The canoe draws closer to the battle, skimming the shallow water and gliding up onto a sandy bar. The clash and clatter of steel, the hum of spears, and the groans of dying men grow louder.

She moves beside her father who parts the folds of the blanket to make a tent over the trembling girl. Peeking out, she watches Lugh jump from the boat and grab hold of the towrope, wading toward shore where two warriors run up the bank. Both wear leather helmets braced with bands of iron and hold shields in their left hands, one the deep red of quicken berries, the other a purplish-brown.

"Lugh, we can't hold them off any longer."

On the edge of Lake Arrow the warriors clash. Off the chests of those who wear leather armor, the arrows fly as if they have hit stone, but the others, who wear only linen tunics that can barely repel the wind, buckle and bleed on the shore.

Then the messenger wretches a stream of blood and falls with a splash at Lugh's feet, a spear still shuddering in his back, while Lugh reaches for the slingshot tucked beneath his belt.

"No, Lugh," the fallen man's companion shouts. "The Tuatha decided that you should not fight. We can't lose you!"

"Better to lose all our kinsmen?"

Lugh leaps onto the rocks that border the lake. Svana looks out and spies through the swirling mist the one-eyed king of the Fomorians, standing high above the battle on an embankment.

"That must be Balor," she whispers to her father, huddling closer to him, welcoming the hollow shelter of his ribs. From beneath the blanket she watches a squat warrior, striding down the shore beside a woman bearing a shield and spear. They near where the boat is moored by the rocks, and Svana sees the glint of the gold bracelets from the woman's forearms and on the man's chest the brooch identical in all but the color of the stone to her own.

"Nuada, stop! Macha, tell him to go back."

"Lugh. You know well that my husband did not lose his hand retreating."

He draws his sword from his scabbard while in the branches of the willow that stretch over the bank, a warrior waits. When Nuada steps beneath, he leaps onto his back, hacking with his short dagger, delivering a quick death to the king whose weapon clatters to the ground. Macha's face contorts with fury. She retrieves the sword, raises it and in one blow splits the skull of her husband's attacker just as a spear pierces her from back to chest.

Lugh springs from the rocks to the side of his fallen kinsmen as the crow he calls Morrigan lands and flaps her wings on the bodies of Macha and Nuada, her gaping beak letting out a furious cry. Lugh speaks to the bird, and though Svana cannot hear his words, she sees the pain wreathing across his brow.

Mark his face. It bears the grief of a man who has lost his friends not once, but every time he has crossed this lake to fight the same battle over and over again, here in the hell of their own making.

Svana watches Lugh stand over the dead assassin and shout.

"Kinsman by birth though you are, I spit on your corpse for

having killed so great a king, beside whom Balor is but a maggot."

Upon hearing the insult Balor speaks. "Lift up my eyelid, that I may see the talkative fellow who so praises me."

Remember what Dagda said. Don't look upon the eye.

Although it is as hard to look away as to look upon the fate of her friend, she draws the blanket over her eyes. "Cover your eyes, too."

I am beyond the harm of phantoms.

He watches as four servants lift the eyelid of Balor. They too must look away as they prop open the gaping hole that houses the pulsing wad of gel and pus. Two warriors fall at the sight of it. Beneath her blanket, she hears the screams of horror that end their lives with an abruptness that can only be delivered by sorcery.

Lugh averts his eyes as he places a black stone in the slingshot that he raises, hurling the stone that finds its mark. It bores a bloody hole in the ogre's head and another as the evil eye flies out the back of his skull, striking down his own men, dismembering them in a spray of gore. The others are retreating over the embankment.

Svana rests her cheek against her father's ribs. The sounds of the phantom warriors driving off the last of their enemies grows faint. Again she hears the caw-cawing of the hooded crow that lands beside her, rocking the boat with the flapping of its wings. In that movement she feels her own weariness overtake her. Sleepily, she recalls the words that Lugh had spoken, the chant of the physician's son, which she now murmurs to herself.

"Joint to joint and sinew to sinew, joint to joint and sinew to sinew." Over and over her words turn like a spindle, making sturdy strands from thin fibers. "Joint to joint and sinew to sinew, joint to joint and sinew to sinew." Over and over she murmurs these words until lulled by the chant and the warmth of the body against which she nuzzles, she falls asleep.

Morrigan's Song

Although gusts of wind batter and pitch the canoe, Svana is warm beneath her blanket and lulled by the movement of the boat. Deeply she sleeps as her mind mends all the tattered bits of stories she has ever heard into one fabric: the pieces woven by her grandmother in the shadows cast by countless turf fires, connecting seamlessly to the patches told by Harte, Queen Maeve, her father, Lugh and Dagda.

When she wakes, she looks out from the boat onto the shore where no trace remains of the battle—no bodies, no weapons, no blood-splattered rocks. Now the Field of Tears is empty and toward it she rows the small boat that in the night has drifted toward the middle of Lough Arrow.

On the shore the warriors and wives of the Tuatha are gathering, their satin mantles flapping in the wind like triumphant flags, striped and checkered and brightly colored. Leading them is Lugh who turns toward the lake.

"Lugh!" she calls, splashing into the shallows and wading toward him, the hem of her wet mantle, weighing her down. "Have you seen my father?"

"He isn't with us."

"But I have to find him."

"Follow that ridge to the *Well of Slane*. It is there the families of the fallen have gone." Reaching into the sleeve of his cloak, he hands her a drawstring bag of dark green silk.

"What's this?"

"Healing herbs gathered from the grave of Miach, slain by his father."

"But Miach saved the King, he brought the Silver Hand to life. Why would his own father kill him?"

"Jealousy, hatred, fear. All that drives us back again and again to fight the same battle and draw the same blood, our own blood, over and over."

The rattling beat of the bodhrán comes from the head of the procession on the shore, and the bagpipes sound one low note and then like a wind gathering force, the music of the instruments come together and carry the procession northward.

"I must go."

The drone of the pipes and lilting, skirling tones swirl above them. Then Lugh's body fades. With each step away from her, substance drains from his form until she can see through his chest a grove of white birches. He crosses toward the Tuatha who appear as thin as the mist that rises from the ground beneath their feet.

"Lugh, don't leave. You have to lead me to Tara. Lugh!"

As the phantoms merge with the mist, Svana feels crushed by all she has lost. The loss of her mother, whose absence she carries in her like a windy hollow, a cavern wide enough to encompass the death of her grandmother and the space above the charred branches of their hut burnt to the ground.

And now the loss of the Tuatha.

Trudging toward the Well of Slane, she cannot feel the sun that has begun to warm the fields around her, but feels only the returning damp chill of her own emptiness, an emptiness that was briefly filled by the friendships she had made on the other side of the lake. How she wishes to rejoin them by the Cauldron of Undry and smell the spices of Dagda's stew rising from it, and hear more of her family's own story. How she wishes to hug Holly again and inhale the scent of her skin, the scent of evergreen nubs plucked from a branch and rubbed between her fingers. And for the first time she misses her father.

Coming to the crest of the hill, Svana is stirred from her self-pity by the sight of the wounded, nursed by the women and children who scurry with rags and buckets and bundles of bread from one injured warrior to the next. Among them she searches for her father.

A boy approaches whose head is wrapped in rags, streaked with the dark stains of blood spilled yesterday and the bright blood that continues to seep through.

"Can you help us?"

In a daze, amid the moans and weeping, Svana follows the boy to a beardless man, his one leg splayed and gashed from calf to thigh while the other is but a stump that bleeds from the knee into the earth. His eyes are glazed, but from his parted lips stirs a breath that bends the blade of grass his son holds before them.

Svana reaches for the bag that Lugh gave her and tugs on its drawstring, releasing a spicy sweet aroma that wafts to the injured man's nostrils which widen as he stirs. She remembers a poultice her grandmother used to make of wild herbs. Then from the nearby well she scoops up the cool water, tinged pink with the blood of the wounded, to dribble on the pile of crushed leaves in her hand. Working the crushed, dampened leaves with her finger into a paste, she dabs it on the open wounds of the outstretched leg. Then with the wide brown leaves of the oak tree, she applies the rest of the dampened herbs to the place where his other leg has been severed. The folds and wrinkles of pain pass from the man's face, his eyes open and his mouth slackens, and the man is instantly healed.

"Thank you, miss," says the boy as he, his father and the hundred kinsmen around them fade into the hillside. Again Svana stands alone, feeling the dull ache of her solitude. With her sadness comes an anger at Queen Maeve who continues to drive her deeper into the ranks of her own family, only to deprive her of them again and again.

Suddenly a tall warrior emerges from a grove of evergreen trees on the edge of the clearing. She bolts toward the woods. But the man chases her and with long strides is quickly upon her. He grabs hold of her long braid and pulls her back, taking hold of her waist.

"Svanhildur."

At the sound of that distant name, she looks up at the man in leather armor beneath a thick, gray woolen cloak. She recognizes first the eyes, one blue and one hazel, then the cropped yellow beard. His hands like hers are bloody from caring for the wounded.

"But how?"

"It was the words you spoke last night, the chant of Miach that restored the Silver Hand, knitting together life and death, so that now I can be your father, and not the shattered demon you knew me to be."

At the Well of Slane they kneel and dip their hands into the water that bubbles up from an underground spring until the current runs clear.

Before the sun is midway across the sky, they make their way back to the place by the rocks where Svana had left the boat that is now no more than a black dab on the lake.

"The boat, it's gone! And our bread!"

"You've not much faith in an old Northman," says her father pulling a coarse thread from the edge of his cloak. "Or the lake that's as generous as Dagda when it comes to feeding friend or foe willing to fish in its water."

"But we can't stop now."

"Who knows what world we'll end up in with each turn that we take. Nature has been generous enough to put a lake before us, and so we'll not turn our back on her hospitality before we set off again."

So Svana sits down on a rock and dips her tired feet into the water, only to be startled by a splash.

"Don't disturb the bank dwellers."

"Fairies?"

"Fairies with fins instead of wings. It's under the bank wild brown trout feed this time of day. But since I no longer have my bony hooks to grab one, we'll have to find some bone to make a gorge."

"What's a gorge?"

"You don't know what a gorge is? And you living in a land of lakes with pike as long as my arm, and you've never even seen a gorge?"

"My father never taught me to fish."

"Well, it's time I did."

They come to the willow tree where Nuada's attacker had hid in its branches. There at the roots they find the bony remains of a badger. Her father takes the bone of what was once its hind leg, then placing it on a flat boulder and wrapping his hand over a rock, he comes down on it with such force that splits it into three pieces. He chooses the one no more half the length of his finger, and chisels its edges. She watches as he sharpens both ends, testing with his own fingertip until a drop of blood proves its readiness.

"See how sharp it is on both ends. Well, we'll cast it out and once the fish grabs hold, with a jerk of my hand it's stuck in its gullet, and with another tug there's more than a tasty morsel for our meal. Now for the shimmer."

"What's a shimmer?"

"It's what catches the fish's eye. Give me the bag."

She hands him the green satin bag that had held the healing herbs, and from it he rips off an edge of its rich fabric. Then he ties the green ribbon around the gorge, and with the long thread from his cloak for a fishing line, he dangles it from between the Y at the end of the birch branch he holds out over the bank where the gorge settles on the surface. Lightly he tugs at the thread which is wrapped around the palm of his hand.

Svana spreads across the smooth rocks to stare into the water where the minnows swim. Dipping down her fingers first to the left of them and then to the right, she pesters the tiny fish. She wonders if Harte is right, and if there is a single will that drives the world, and if it's driving them in the same way for its own amusement. Suddenly a speckled trout flaps wildly by her side on the bank.

Her father grabs the tail of the dappled fish and brings its head down hard on the boulder. Then removing the gorge from its gullet, he cuts open its belly and removes its entrails. Soon she is sitting holding the long, mottled fish impaled on a branch over a fire. Her mouth waters as its skin crisps and crackles. Finally, she draws the skewered fish from the fire close to her nostrils to inhale its aroma then bites down, burning her tongue and spitting the hot chunk onto the palm of her hand. She blows on it for a moment then pops it back into her mouth and chews the succulent morsel. As she licks her fingers, the sound of splashing draws her attention to the lake.

Not far from shore, a family of swans is crossing the lake when with its wings unfurled, a cob attacks. The angry swan treads the water with its webbed feet beating the surface. The defending male rises in retaliation. Groaning and hissing they fight near where the boat has drifted back toward shore when suddenly the cob charges toward the two swanlings. Nabbing one in its beak, it forces its head underwater. Svana grabs a stone from the bank and throws it toward the attacker.

"Stop. He's drowning it."

The skirt of her mantle floats around her like a water lily as she wades into the lake, hurling more stones. But the battle ends as the cob releases the limp body of the blue-grey cygnet, and its parents swim off with one surviving offspring.

Then the swan approaches the boat where a length of purple fabric hangs over the side. It snatches a corner of the blanket and tugs it off into the water before disappearing below the surface of the lake.

"That's mine! My blanket and my brooch." Furiously, she splashes deeper into the water.

"Svanhildur, stop. Born of fire and frost, swans come from emptiness and will lead you only to the place of the dead."

"I have to get them."

"Not at the price of crossing the border that divides this world from the ones below. I traveled that way once, and there is no bottom."

He crosses into the lake to carry her back struggling. Sitting her down on the shore, he stretches his arm around her sagging shoulders.

"But I want them back."

"It's not the blanket or the brooch. It's her you miss. But she's with you still. I hear her in your voice when you scold. I see her in that red hair and that tough nature of yours."

"Will I ever see her again?"

"I never believed the stories my grandmother told me or the old nags reading the runes. But my journeys after death have taken me through mist and fire to know their truth. And they used to say that in the end we meet again, all the ancestors back to the beginning of time."

"Then I want this life to be over."

"Death doesn't come for the asking, and it may be a hundred journeys more we must make before the reward of the end of time comes to us."

The hooded crow settles on a stump beside them and caws loudly. Svana hurries toward the bird. "It's the crow Lugh calls Morrigan. Maybe she can lead us to him."

They follow the bird as spreading its wide wings it flies northward out of sight and then settles on a branch and caws until they catch up to her.

They travel until dusk overtakes the hills when not far off on a high ridge, a procession of phantoms is moving toward a monument of stone. Svana knows that it is the Tuatha bearing the King and Queen toward their tomb dug into the hillside. At its entrance a massive slab is set atop the arm-like pillars of stone that seem to be reaching out of the ground to pull the Dé Dannan below the earth.

Their legs do not move as they float like swirling columns of smoke above the ground. The sound of the beats of the bodhrán seem to draw them toward the *dolmen* where Nuada and his Queen will be laid to rest. A glint of light bounces off his Silver Hand.

"We have to reach them before they enter the tomb!" cries Svana. Her father bends down on one knee, and she hops on his back. She holds tightly as he runs, but the closer they get, the fainter the phantom procession becomes. Finally when they are within a few feet of the Tuatha, one by one, the warriors and their wives disappear into the hillside, fading beneath the stones of the portal and into the earth. Just as Lugh proceeds to enter, Svana leaps to the ground.

"Lugh, wait!"

But they have already passed through the stones into the invisible abyss of the tomb as the crow speaks.

"This is the tomb of Nuada and the portal to that underground world where the Dé Dannan will dwell for all time as the *ban* and *fershee*, the men and women of the hill."

"But the Silver Hand. We're doomed without it."

The crow circles above their heads. "Look beside the stones." Svana crosses to a mossy mound where rests the Silver Hand as her father kneels and lifts the gleaming object.

"Truly, Goibniu was a great smith."

Shifting restlessly on her father's palm, three silver fingers bend inward while like an arrow one finger shoots out. Then rising the hand spins, hovering above their heads until it stops midair and points eastward.

The crow settles on a low branch.

"It's toward Tara you must travel."

And then slowly descending, like a body separating from its soul, the solid silver form forged by Goibnu releases a silver shadow as the metal hand flies toward the same portal through which its owner has passed.

"Stop the Hand! Maeve said I have to bring it to her."

"Have no fear. Its spirit will lead you to another warrior, a descendant of Nuada, who will take you to your journey's end. As for Maeve, the Tuatha will deal with her at the final *feish*."

"What feast?"

"The final feish where the Tuatha has gathered, awaiting your arrival to bridge the lands of legend and life, so that all may pass onto a new era of peace."

"Why don't you show us the way?"

"Because I must follow my generation under the hills where we will dwell for all time, undisturbed by the battles that rock the earth."

Then a wind stirs, taking with it the black feathers of the crow whose shape shifts into that of a tiny woman. She wears a gown that is white and edged in black with a tiny dark hood flowing over her narrow shoulders. From her back sprouts wings, as fine as dewy cobwebs woven between twigs. Tilting back her head, the fairy chants a song of farewell before flying off and fading into the hillside.

> *"Peace up to heaven, and from heaven to earth,*
> *A cup full of honey to welcome each birth*
> *Summer in winter and joy in the Hall,*
> *An abundance of peace I wish to you all!"*

"And peace to you, Morrigan," calls Svana, holding her father's hand as they head back to the shore of Lough Arrow where throughout the night the spirit of the Silver Hand hovers above the tree branches and fades with the dawn.

Abduction of Sabd

An acorn drops from the paw of the *togmall* that stands on the lowest branch of the tree, chattering at the large furless animal off whose head it bounces. Startled awake by the rap on her brow, Svana reaches for the nut that rolls to the ground and flings it back at the pestering creature that leaps down onto her mossy bed to scold her even more fiercely.

"So, we have a guest." Her father smiles, setting down a birch-bark platter lined with leaves of watercress on which he has piled the red berries of the rowan and the tart, purple sloes of the blackthorn along with the sweet nuts that he has gathered and shelled from the hazel tree.

"I've no hospitality for one so rude." Popping a pale hazelnut into her mouth, she savors its buttery flavor, following with a quick succession of berries while the togmall at her feet continues to protest.

"According to the law of your own people, even outlaws are due lodging and a meal."

"Then let the forest feed him." Svana's eyes narrow as the intruder lurches forward with a burst of speed toward the breakfast platter. It grabs two nuts, putting one into each cheek, before scurrying back up the trunk and into the branches.

"Good riddance," she shouts at the chattering head that

pops out of a rotted gap in the tree.

"Togmalls are plentiful in the forests to the east, and wild things far fiercer."

"In Sligo Mamó said that the men of the village used to set out with their hounds to hunt the wolves that attacked their sheep, so I never went far from the sea for fear of them in the hills."

"Not to worry, lass. I'm a match for any enemy on four legs or two. Finish your meal. The sooner we set out, the sooner we'll come to the end of this journey."

They start off, walking eastward from the northern shore of Lough Arrow. In the hours that pass, the broader the distance they put between themselves and the Plain of Tears, the dimmer the memory becomes of the warriors who battled there, and in the days that follow, they walk and walk, putting lakes and fields and the thick acres of a dense forest between them and the shades of witches, gods and war.

Nor do they speak of the Silver Hand that has kept them on this eastward course, nor of their encounters with Dagda, Lugh or Bridey. They waste little time on conversation as they travel, for the demands of crossing this primordial terrain means they have to keep their minds alert to their own survival. It is as if that other world faded when the shades of those Celtic warriors slipped beneath the archway of rocks north of Lough Arrow, the gods diminishing in their minds to no more than stories told in childhood.

Instead they speak only of the many ways her father teaches her to survive: how to lash together a rough raft or build a shelter against a gathering storm, how to hunt, to fish and to forage. Although it takes many cuts and bruises on her fingers, she masters making a spearhead. He shows her how to chip away ridges from a stone core into the blades of flint that she then shapes and sharpens to a lethal edge.

It is on the day when the last leaves rattle on the hardwood trees that Svana carries the shaft of her first spear through the forest, creeping stealthily behind her father. When he steps aside, she knows it is time to raise her weapon, to aim and hurl, the moment she has sighted the prey.

She is about to let fly her spear when there comes a low piteous moan just beyond the bushes. Dropping the spear to her side, she approaches and sees the great stag sagging heavily from between two ash trees, its massive rack of antlers ensnared in the grip of the hardwood branches.

With a jab to its heart her father ends its pain. With none of the excitement or pride she felt when she landed her first salmon or brought down a wild bird with her slingshot, she helps her father bring the carcass to the ground. He boosts her into the ash tree, climbing up behind her so they can pry back the interlocking branches. The animal falls with a crack and a heavy thud. Looking down at its vast body, Svana wonders how no animal has mauled the beast as it dangled there.

"Even half alive he'd still have had such fight in him that his flailing hooves and savage snorts would have driven them off."

He then sets to work skinning, gutting, butchering and smoking meat of the hefty beast to preserve it for the winter ahead.

While he works, Svana's place has been by the fire, careful not to let the flames catch the low hanging branches while she keeps her torch smoldering to ward off predators.

On the third evening of tending the fire her mind wanders back to the shores of Sligo, unaware that a wild cat has dropped from a low branch and furtively moves toward the fire. Its shoulders hunched low to the ground, it sights its target, the small human that appears to be dozing by the fire.

A prickly sensation runs across her shoulders and up her scalp. Roused from her daydreaming, she turns with alarm to see the cat poised and ready to pounce. His prey now alert, the bobcat springs. Dropping the torch, she rolls out of its range, her eyes locked with the wild cat's amber glare. Just as she inhales with terror, her father leaps over the fire and grabs the torch, his feet slamming the ground with a force that matches the maniacal cry that bellows from him.

For a moment, stunned by the newness of such behavior from any prey, the cat lingers until a jab of the torch singes its fur and with a growl of pain, the animal runs back deep into the woods.

"Keep closer watch," her father growls, handing back the torch.

Returning to the pit he has dug and covered with branches and leaves, he smokes the long thin strands of meat. For the remaining days at their makeshift camp, the smell of roasting venison overpowers the smell of pines, and they eat their fill of fresh meat. Her father tries to get her to taste the mash he has made of the brains, but she declines, preferring the grilled loins and tender steaks without muscle or gristle from the diaphragm. On such fare Svana feels a strength she has never known on the vegetables and grains she ate back home, with an occasional stew of Harte's ocean harvest.

While the remaining slabs of meat absorb the smoke of the oak branches, her father carves an awl from one of the antlers. She watches him punch out holes down the length of his rough gray cloak. Unraveling a length of thread from its edge, he sews up three sides to make a pack to store the dried meat. Growing restless, Svana wanders off to explore. She finds bushes of the red berries that appear to be rose hips and picks the tiny hard beads that bounce on the fabric of the mantle that she holds before her like a basket. She carries them back to the campsite to boil them down to make her grandmother's tonic.

Walking along, she pops a handful into her mouth, swallows and then gags. She spits out the poisonous fruit, but her stomach has already begun to cramp. By the time she reaches the fire, she is doubled over in pain. Her father runs to lift her up and lie her down on her bed of branches. There for two days he hovers over her, dosing her with a warm brew of wild blackberries and the bitter leaves of the sorrel until on the third day she arises, ready to resume their journey.

Despite the hardship of their travels, she enjoys the life outdoors and companionship of her father. She likes the sureness of his fingers as he carves a gorge or guts a fish; she likes the yellow and silver hair that carpets his forearm, but most of all she likes his smell, a saltiness that reassures her.

When her father tells stories of his childhood, curiosity replaces her fear of the North. He tells her of Iceland and the volcano he watched erupt while standing in the yard of the long house from which he and his grandmother's family had to flee. His daughter learns too that he named her after the mother he had barely known and that he too had been raised by his grandmother. Only as a man did he learn that he was fathered by Turgeis, who had sailed from Denmark and sired the sons and daughters for whom he had no more concern than the peasant girls who gave birth to them.

Svana's father tells of how when he reached his own

restless manhood, there being no land for him to till, he traveled to Norway and sailed on the Northman long ships. His daughter knows not to ask him any questions, to accept what of his own life he is willing to share. But it is in those stories that she finds something of herself, her own rugged nature and love of the sea.

So they travel, content with their own company until one night, after they have made camp on the eastern edge of the forest, they are awakened by the rustling of approaching hooves. Silently they rise from their rustic beds and listen to the strange gurgling coming from under a bush.

Her father aims his spear. Then with a rush of air the spear barely misses the doe that vaults, its white tail tipping toward the moon. But instead of disappearing deeper into the woods, the animal stops and stares back at them. As Svana moves toward the babbling bush, the deer's eyes follow her.

She steps forward to part the branches to reveal the source of the sound. On the ground sits a child no more than two years of age, a sturdy, naked boy whose fawn-like eyes meet hers with neither recognition nor fear, regarding her with the same blank curiosity with which he might examine a bird or bright stone. Spittle bubbles from his lips as he reaches up for the girl now crouching above him. She is surprised at the strength of the baby who wraps his arms around her neck and pulls her closer to him.

Encircling the baby's back with both her arms, she lifts him to her chest where with vigorous instinct he nuzzles and snuffles, demanding to be fed.

"Oh, no," she says, shifting him onto her hip and then holding the baby out to her father.

The baby drools and babbles up at the stranger, grabbing

hold of the shaft of his spear.

"Is it a warrior you'll be, lad? Or by the sound of your babbling, maybe it's a poet or worse still a Brehon."

"Who would leave a baby in these woods?"

"He's not alone." He nods toward the doe that cautiously approaches. When the baby reaches out its arms, the animal quickens its step and comes to him, her rough tongue brushing back the black curls from his forehead and then licking the fawn colored skin of his cheeks with all the tenderness of a mother. Onto the doe's back he places the squirming baby that straddles her neck and hugs tightly. They watch the deer step away, the boy swaying with her lithe rhythm, stopping every few feet along the way and lifting her muzzle to beckon them.

Twigs and dry leaves crackling beneath their feet, they follow to a swamp overgrown with rushes and sedge below a steep ridge. Sure-footedly the doe crosses the fen from rock to rotten stump with Svana and her father slogging their way through the muddy bog and thick ferns.

When they come to the rocky slope, the doe is treading a familiar path and rises from one narrow ledge to the next, each time looking behind with a nod of her head. Step by narrow, rocky step she climbs, chunks of earth tumbling to the ground beneath her faltering feet. Reaching the top of the ridge, she shimmies over and looks down at her father who is still stumbling, trying to gain his footing.

"It's a path fit for a goat or a girl. I'll come from behind the ridge."

"Hurry," she calls, her voice drowned out by the waterfall that rings off the nearby rocks and into a moon-bright pool. Peeling off her leather slippers, she feels the tender new grass around its edge, cool and slick and moist beneath her feet, and follows the doe to where the water parts from the wall of the ravine. There the doe and child slip behind the tumbling cascade.

In this cool recess of rock and moss, the doe bends forward on its front legs so that the baby rolls down onto a bed of pine needles beneath a cushion of leaves and dry grass. The doe nudges the natural coverlet into soft mounds around the boy who weary from the night's wandering, utters a faint whimper before falling asleep almost as quickly as Svana.

At dawn she is awakened by the pummeling of two chubby feet against her ribs. Rolling over, she notices that the deer is gone.

She moves to the mouth of their dwelling and watches the doe with her head bent, drinking from the misty pool. About to cross over, Svana stops at the sight of a man coming over the rise. He is a slight man with a sunken face and sharp eyes that stare intently at the doe.

Her hearing dimmed by the churning water, the doe does not at first notice the interloper who stalks her from behind. But when he stands beside her and removes a branch of the hazelnut tree from the sleeve of his robe, the tension that overtakes her muscles conveys her fear. Before she can bound off, he touches her with the wand and bewitches her into a trance. Her proud head dips downward, and she follows the druid back over the edge of the ridge.

Svana steps behind the watery veil. Unaware of any danger, the baby lolls on his grassy bed, sucking his toes while she wonders what she will do if the wizard comes back for the boy. Hours pass and still there is no sign of her father. The baby begins to cry with hunger, so she lifts and rocks him, more for her own comfort than his. Suddenly a rough-nosed intruder nudges her elbow.

When she jumps to her feet, the baby tumbles from her lap beneath the legs of the nanny goat that now stands beside them. The baby, having caught sight of her dripping teats, immediately grows quiet and suckles greedily on all fours as her father enters their hideaway.

"Where have you been?"

"I saw a hut on the other side of the ridge. In it was an old woman who was more than willing to trade this nanny for our smoked elk. Where's the doe?"

"She's been taken."

"Taken?"

"By a druid, I could tell by the hazel wood wand and the way he bewitched her."

"Show me the way they went."

Svana reaches down for the baby who has fallen back contentedly, milk dribbling down his cheeks and chest, belching loudly as the goat nibbles at his bed. Crossing out of the cave, she points over to the edge of the ridge.

"Wait here with the babe. Gods and demons I was powerless against, but a druid's no more than a man, and his only power is our fear. And I am finished with fear."

Hurling himself off the ridge, he hits the ground with a thud, springs to his feet and waves up to her before taking off at a run.

"The only fear I have is being left to care for you," she mutters, trying to wrest her nose from the fierce twisting grip of the baby. The morning dew glistens on the grass with a beauty that is lost to Svana who keeps one eye on the boy and one on the angle of the sun.

Throughout the day the toddler plays, displaying unusual strength and dexterity—hurling rocks across the glade, catching dragonflies and racing away from Svana who by evening can no longer keep up with him. Finally exhausted by his own antics, and having helped himself to a final feeding beneath the nanny, the toddler falls onto his stomach, fast asleep with his milky lips ajar.

Anxious for her father's return, she lifts the baby and follows a path through the tall grass, hoping to see or hear a sign of his approach. Above her stretches the dusky sky where against a bank of grey clouds the silvery shadow of the hand reappears and points in the direction of the woods beyond the clearing from which echo sharp yaps and howls.

Frightened by the fierce racket, she hurries back toward the shelter of the lair. Slowed down by the weight of the baby, she makes her way to the water's edge with the fierce baying of the pack of animals drawing near.

Svana trips, one ankle twisting beneath her. The baby jolted awake by the icy water, howls more loudly than the dogs that surround them baring their teeth. She reaches for a rock, ready to slam down on the nose of whichever mongrel attacks when one dog, long-legged as a colt with a bristly coat of gray fur, takes the lead and snarls at the pack. The hunting dogs draw back as the wolfhound growls, bracing itself to lunge at the first dog to challenge his leadership.

A rider approaches. Swinging from his saddle is a man, broader and taller than any mortal she has ever met. His face is barely visible beneath a fiery beard that blazes up over his ears and flares up the side of his face. He wears his hair in a long, neat braid that runs over his shoulder. He holds the bridle of his sorrel horse whose hide glints with sparks of red and flecks of silvery gray. The massive dog that stands as tall as his waist trots to his side.

He strikes out with his riding crop into the pack of dogs whose pink gums and white fangs gleam. "Back, mangy curs." Goaded into submission by his curses and the snarling threats of the wolfhound, the pack backs off. "Good job, Brann. Keep 'em back!"

The man dismounts and wades toward the girl and baby. He scoops up the child, cradling him in one arm as he extends a thick, callused hand to Svana. Grimacing, she stumbles back onto dry ground where he slips off her leather *cuarán* and examines her ankle.

"To be sure, it's twisted as a torque, but not broken."

Fascinated by the stranger's beard, the toddler grips an orange tendril and yanks down hard. The man howls, but the baby squeals with delight. He sets the baby down beside the girl.

He unknots his long silk neckerchief and, wrapping it around the arch of her foot, winds it around her injured ankle, binding it with a firm knot.

"So this brat's your brother?"

"He's no relation to me. My father and I came upon him in the woods, just the other side of this ridge."

"In the woods. A child alone?"

"Odd as it might sound, he was tended by a doe."

The man's eyes turn a darker gray. "Go on."

"She groomed him as if he were her own fawn, and put him down to sleep with the tenderness of a mother."

"Sabd," the man utters to himself. "Where is she now?"

"A druid came. He carried a hazel wood branch, and he lured her away. I didn't know how to stop him."

The stranger loosens his grip. "What strength does a child have against the sorcery that has confounded my men of the *Fianna*?"

"And who are you?"

"Finn MacCool, and it's the life of my own son that you've saved," he says of the baby who is picking up pebbles and dropping them down the Fenian's muddy boot. "And it's your news of his mother that gives me hope."

"How can this be?

"His mother is *Sabd*, my beloved, shifted from her human form by that same wizard who you're after seeing bewitch her once again." Finn, reaches down to pick up his son. "And it was in the forest I first set eyes on a doe so lovely, I called my dogs off and ended the chase. That night she came to me in her true form as a woman who was as beautiful to me as I was to her. And so for a time we lived together, but then one day I was called to Dubh Linn with my men to fight off the attack of the Northmen.

And it was then that our happiness ended. The wizard, whom she had long ago rejected, returned to cast his spell on her to change her back into a four-legged creature that he led away into the forest. I knew from other hunters that she had escaped because they'd seen her in this forest with a baby boy on her back, but it's only now I have the joy of seeing my own son."

The dogs bark as a score of other riders gallop across the glen. "These are the Fianna, my comrades. For months they searched with me for Sabd. And this," he tells them, "is my son."

"Can you be sure, Finn?" asks one rider.

"If I didn't have the boy in my arms, I'd lay you flat with

one blow. I know by the eyes that he belongs to Sabd." Then kisses the baby's forehead. "After her, I'll call you *Oisin*, little fawn."

Oisin yanks again on the beard of his father who after prying his fingers from it places him in the arms of his bewildered companion.

"And what is it you want me to do with him?"

"Care for him until I return."

"Finn," he groans as the other men laugh. "Ask me to board a Northman long ship and lay down the lot of them with my bare hands, but not this!" Deaf to the Fenian's pleas, Finn mounts his sorrel mare and nods for another man to help Svana into the saddle of the black steed. "Ah, Finn, not my horse!"

"Not to worry, man, you'll not be going far, what with the babe to care for till I get back." The newly named Oisin leans closer to the face of his guardian who strains to pull his head beyond the baby's reach. The man yowls in pain as the baby pinches his cheek between his vice like fingers.

"Finn, anything. But don't leave me with the baby!"

"An Irishman in need can always depend on the help of the Fenians," he shouts over the peals of laughter that rise from the men as Finn rides off with Svana, leaving his band of fighters to the harshest ordeal they have yet encountered—caring for Oisin.

Fer Leath

Behind the horse of Finn MacCool, Svana follows on the Fenian's mare. Although Finn often stops to run his fingers along the ground and sniff the air to detect the smell of Sabd, they ride out of the forest without finding a trail. Then they cross the plains until in the distance appears a flat-topped hill on which rises a tall and ambling building, constructed of timbers carved and painted in bold colors.

"Is that Tara?" she asks, remembering Queen Maeve's words and hoping that they are nearing the end of their journey.

"What put a thought like that in your head? Tara's been the palace of the High Kings since before man put marks on stone. That's just my own house."

"So that's where you live."

"Never more than nine nights in a row."

"Why only nine?

"For one I prefer the forest and the plains and the open sky over my head when I sleep. And when the weather's foul there's always the hospitality of all the Irish farm folk who put fresh rushes on the floor and extra meat on the spit when we're in need of a night's lodging. For another it'd be bad luck."

"How is it bad luck to sleep in your own bed?"

"It's just a *geasa* and I'm not to do it."

"What's a geasa?"

"Jaysus, but it's more questions you have, girl, than there are wolves in all Ireland."

"I just want to know."

"It's just that some things are harder to explain."

"Can't you try?"

"Well, a geasa is a sort of prohibition. And if you don't mind it, bad luck will befall you. Like walking about on the eve of Samhain."

"I didn't used to believe that, but I do now. But why would there be a geasa not to sleep in your own house?"

"Think about it. I'm the head of the Fenians. If I go and get myself too comfortable by my own hearth, I might not be ready when the call came to defend Ireland. And my men, the Fianna? If they sat around the long winter from *Samhain* to *Imbolc*, they'd grow lazy and fat, and they'd not be inclined to move at all, now would they?"

"So, you're a kind of army?"

"Don't go confusing the Fianna with any rag tag bunch of rent payers a local Chieftain calls up every time his neighbor's thugs are at his doorstep. The Fenians are the finest trained of all defenders."

"How do you know you're the best?"

"We accept no man until a hole's been dug, and he put in it to his waist. And with only his shield and a branch of hazel the length of his arm, he must defend himself against nine men who stand ten furrows width apart and assail him with their spears."

"Nine men throwing spears at one man in a hole. That's no fair match."

"Life is no fair match, lassie. What with all the elements of the earth; water, wind, air and fire conspiring to take us underground to keep company with the roots of trees, at least we Fenians give a man a fighting chance."

"But what if he can't fend off nine men?"

"You mean if he dies?"

"Yes, what if he dies?"

"Then he's no Fenian."

"Has a woman ever been a Fenian?"

"It's the women who have too much sense for fighting. What with the real work of the world, they've little time for such nonsense."

"So, you're saying what you do is nonsense?"

"I'm only saying I do what I do because I was born Finn MacCool, a son of *Cumal*, head of the Fianna before me. And neither in his time nor mine has any woman ever spoken of wanting to be buried waist deep in a hole and having spears thrown at her."

"What other tests of nonsense must a man take to be a Fenian?"

"His agility and speed must be proven as well."

"Do you race?"

"Aye, we Fenians love to race: horses, hounds, curraghs, chariots. Sometimes chariots against curraghs, the one the shore and the other gliding along the lake. But for a man to prove himself a Fenian, he'd have to be able to run through the woods in the dead of night and come out the other side without catching a single hair of his braid on the low hanging branches."

"Back home I have a friend named Harte who says that real strength is in wisdom."

"Aye, we strengthen our minds as well, by memorizing the

tales that are the mark of a learned man."

"So if fighting is nonsense, why do you do it then?"

"Sure, but I'll welcome the day when the Fenians can hang up our shields in the Halls of Tara, and we can lounge at our ease."

"How far off is that?"

"The day when we'll be free to live at our own leisure? There's no telling how long off it will be before mankind comes to its senses."

"It was Queen Maeve who said the Silver Hand would guide me to the Halls of Tara and that's where my journey would end."

"Maeve of Connaught, dead and buried these long centuries since she duped Connaught into war? The no-good lying, greedy Maeve who sent Irish men to their slaughter all because she wanted the Brown Bull of Cooley for herself?"

"Who'd go to war over a bull?"

"I'm telling you that's how vain and witless the woman was. Blood was spilled on both sides, and Ulster's greatest warrior was lost, all for a side of beef."

"Why did she want it so badly?"

"Brainless greed and nothing more. It all started in her own bed when she and Ailill were settling in for the night. Says she to him, I've more wealth than you. Says he to her, nay, you have not. Says she to him, you're wrong. Says he to her, you're daft. So right then in the middle of the night she wakes her servants and has them bring every coin, every cow and jewel that each of them owns, so that she can prove she has more wealth than her husband.

Well, by the time the sun came up, Aillil had won the wager with his prize white bull. This infuriated Maeve. She didn't like to lose. So it was straight away to Ulster that she sent her men to bargain for the famous Brown Bull of Cooley. And, sure wasn't the King ready to close on the deal when Maeve's men went boasting in his hall that they'd have taken it anyway. When the king heard this from his own servants, he called it off and kept his bull. And so Maeve up and went to war."

"Did she get the Brown Bull?"

"Through trickery, deceit and dark alliances, aye, she managed to steal it, and plunge decent folk into battle and turmoil to satisfy her own vanity and greed."

They come to the timber house where an iron gate creaks in its frame and no smoke rises from its chimneys. Svana shivers with the damp chill that envelops the grand, but lifeless estate.

"What's this? No one about, and the hearth's cold? It's a good fire that keeps the timbers dry. My servants have never let the flames die before."

Cautiously, they approach, their horses crossing the wide lawn that surrounds the house. When from the south a dry wind blows, Svana's horse pulls back. Its ears stiffen and tilt forward as its nostrils flare.

Then as if it is a living thing, the house groans. Its walls painted red, green and blue glow more intensely as the air blows hotter, and the sky shuttles back and forth between darkness and dawn. Finn and Svana pull the horses back beyond the low hedge. There in stunned silence they watch as with the heat, the timbers of his house crack, and the wind sweeps up the flecks of fading paint that fly in a vortex over the lawn.

Before their eyes, the bare wide planks and beams, consumed by invisible flames, turn gray then black, and the once sturdy structure tumbles into a heap of charred timbers.

The debris of wood continues to disintegrate into a pile of white ash that the same hot wind takes southward.

"This must be the work of the sorcerer," says Finn. "Or else it is a trick of time that tumbles down a great hall in the flash of an eye."

Then from the smoke that lingers over the stone foundation of the destroyed house, a strand of silver takes on the form of a hand that beckons to them.

"Stop. Don't be foolish, girl," shouts Finn as she follows. But the phantom hand has taken hold of the bridle of his horse and leads him through the smoke behind her and into another age.

The silver shadow leads them over a hill where a patchwork of small plots is marked by low stone walls and planted with a crop whose tiny purple flowers she does not recognize. Though the cottages are thatched as her own was, none are curved. They are rectangular and painted white, far outnumbering those that had dotted the hills of Sligo.

Riding past a battered and tilting shed, Svana wrinkles her nose at the foul smell that rises from a pile of rotting vegetation. A dog with protruding ribs and sunken stomach skulks past them through a grey and putrid mist creeping along the ground. The wispy hand then releases the bridle of Finn's horse before snapping its phantom fingers and like a bubble bursts.

Silently, they ride as the sky grows calm and the hills begin to look familiar. Svana notices that the yards are teeming with scantily dressed children, and that the fields are dotted by so many men and women working side by side, she wonders if perhaps this vastly-populated province is inhabited by the

BOOK TWO

dead of Ireland. What might have been a sad thought, fills her with a sudden hope. For if they have come to the land of the dead, in it she might find her grandmother.

"Are they dead?" she asks Finn whose horse rides beside hers. Finn laughs and points toward the spongy wetland of decayed wood and vegetation where a throng of men and women labor. They cut the blue-black turf with their sharp edged, long-handled *slaans* into slippery sods which they pass to the children who lay them out in rows to dry and harden in the sun.

"Was it a hard day's work?"

"Many—when it was just Harte and I that was cutting it."

"And do you not think that if they be dead, they'd not be working half so hard? For if it's Tirnanóg you've come to, wouldn't it be as June always with no need to labor at all? Hey," the Fenian calls to an old man who stands in his doorway, gazing out at the passing strangers. "The girleen here's after wondering if you're all dead."

"It's dead we'll all be if *Fer Leath* returns."

"Is Fer Leath a Northman?" asks Svana, thinking perhaps the town had been the target of a Northman scourge.

"No Northman ship ever sailed from this coast having caused more harm. For every slave a Northman dragged off or Irishman slain, the Fer Leath's killed a thousand and like to kill ten times more if he walks this way again."

"But how can one warrior kill so many?"

The man steps from behind the low wall. Gaunt and crooked in his gait, he approaches Finn's horse, looks up at its rider and whispers, "Has the poor girl had the madman's wisp blown into her face?"

Finn bends his head down close to the old man's ear. "Aye,

she's mad. Why the lass is just after telling me she's been sent to Tara by Queen Maeve herself."

"It's in these hard times that those who've lost their wits suffer least."

"Aye, true enough. But tell me, who's this Fer Leath fella?"

"Ah, you don't mean to be telling me you've not heard of the Fer Leath?"

"We're new to these parts."

"There's not a man alive in all Ireland that's not heard of the Gray Man, the vile creature who moves under the devil's own fog, a mist so loathsome the stench of it will foul your dreams, and that only if you can sleep. What with the dogs that be barking in a fury through the night, few Irishmen sleep while your man walks the fields, who with a touch of his twisted finger withers the stalks and turns the praties black beneath his cloven hooves."

"So, is it Satan himself has come to Ireland?"

"Nay, it's a descendant of hell far worse than any's ever walked this or any other world. For even as we dug up the potatoes black and oozing from the ground, didn't he find our stores from the last harvest and rot them where they lay beneath the straw, our only hope in the hard months ahead." The old man steps back from the horse and rider and behind the low wall. "And who is it I'd be speaking to that hasn't heard of the fiend who's bedeviled his own people?"

"Don't worry, old man. I'm as true a man as any Fenian."

"I can see that by the look of you, though your clothes and plaited hair be odd for these times. And not many among us still have a nag to ride let alone such fine mares."

"Now why wouldn't any Irish man or woman take pride upon the back of the horses nature has seen fit to be bred on

BOOK TWO

our own island?"

"Sure, but you must have been clobbered in the skull yourself with the butt of a Red Coat's musket, to be talking such foolishness," says the man shaking his head with disbelief. "That or the two of you have been living with the fairies under the hill not to know that the very horses we've bred have been taken from us, like our own land and our own sweet mother tongue."

"I don't understand. Who can take from you who you are?"

"Truly, it's to fairies I must be talking. Though I've no fear of you, being a *shanachie* myself when I still had the heart to conjure a tale and the mind to remember it. I've always been a great friend of the little people."

"Maybe it's not too far off the mark that you are, old man. But surely you're right not to fear us as we may be strangers, but we're as true an Irishman and lass as ever you'll meet on this or any shore."

"Then come in. For if my wits, which in these terrible times do go roaming back to better times, haven't left me completely, I've still a sup of *poteen* hidden away in the hearth that I'd not be wasting on the likes of you."

"Poteen?"

"Poteen, man. Now don't be telling me you never had a sup of the bottle to ease your troubles."

"It's plenty of comfort I've found in a goblet of good ale or *míd*, but poteen I've never heard of before."

"There's not a living man in all Ireland who could make that claim, stranger." The old man shuffles toward the cottage. Finn dismounts and raises his arms to catch Svana who slides off the saddle to follow him and the old man into the bare hovel that is his home. "Dark times do be on us, surely," he mutters to himself. "What with a wife and daughter dead, and two fine sons gone off to foreign lands, is it any wonder that it's fairies I'd be talking to?"

On the patched knees of his trousers he kneels by the hearth in which no fire is lit. Reaching up into the chimney he feels around with his hand, frustration filling the cracks and creases of his old face. "My mind does be playing tricks on me sometimes. I'm sorry I've nothing better to offer than water from the well."

"Look again, old man."

And this time when his wizened hand, scratching about the ash and cinders, comes upon a clay bottle that he draws out and displays to his guests, his face brightens. With what teeth he has left, the old man yanks out the cork that gives way with a sleek pop, and with that first gulp coursing down his gullet, his eyes moisten with a gleam that spills over his gnarled features.

"Why, blessed be the saints of all Ireland, it's full!" he exclaims before crossing to a narrow cobwebbed shelf where two tin cups are set. Blowing off the dust, his shaking hand offers one to each guest, filling both to the brim.

Svana surveys the room, not so very different than the inside of her hut, but barren and unkempt, with only the old milking stool on which she sits, a few old feed bags and a filthy blanket in the corner.

"*Sláinte*," says Finn who raises his cup and slugs down his drink, his eyes widening as the poteen sears his throat and fills his chest with a fire that shows in his now-blazing eyes.

"That's ten times ten the strength of any míd or ale."

"Sure ale's no match for whiskey, man, and it's in these hard times a sup of either is as rare as a coin in an Irishman's pocket." The old man raises his glass and tips back his drink. "But still there's nothing like a sup of the bottle can set the insides afire and bring the old times back to life."

"Aye," agrees Finn as he refills his cup.

"Now go on, take a sip, lass. Sure, it'll ease the weariness of your travels."

Not wanting to decline the old man's hospitality, she takes the gray cup from his hand. In the shadows of the cottage, the poteen looks murky, like a dark pool beneath the overhanging limbs of the dense forest through which they have passed. Raising the cup to her lips, she sips the home brewed whiskey. It runs over her tongue and she gags slightly, surprised that the poteen burns more than it tastes, a flame trailing down her throat as a quiver runs through her. She passes the cup back to her aged host.

"Thank you," she sputters, "but no more."

"There's not a man in Ireland would let a good cup of poteen go to waste. Sláinte!" He tips back her unfinished drink. Then wasting no time, he refills both his cup and Finn's.

Already the poteen causes her to sway on the stool as the room spins around her.

"You look fit to fall over," says Finn steadying the girl.

"I am a bit tired," she murmurs, looking toward the ragged mass of dirty cloth in the corner. Finn moves away from the hearth where he stands and, taking off his own wool coat, spreads it atop the filthy pile.

Swaying, Svana crosses to the makeshift bed and curls up on the rich satin lining of Finn's great coat, inhaling the warmth of it and the smell of fresh hay mingling with the reassuring scent of her own father. She tucks her hands beneath her cheek and feels her body sink, the soreness of her muscles from the ride slipping away as the warmth of the poteen overtakes her. But she does not sleep. Closing her eyes, she listens, as certain as when her grandmother prepared to tell a tale, that a story is in the air.

"So, what's your name, man?"

"Owen Reilly, Descendant of Raghlach, chiefs of Brefne, breeders of fine horses. Sure, but we've known better times."

"It's many a Reilly has ridden with the Fianna and rare was the rogue among them. But isn't it far from your own fair hills of Cavan you've come to settle here in Kildare."

"It's hard times that have driven us from home, but sure no one knows the land and the families that are in it better than you, Finn MacCool."

"And how is it that you know me, man?" slurs Finn, setting down his drink on the mantle shelf and staring at his host in amazement.

"Are you not after telling me that it's with the Fianna you ride?"

"It's the poteen that must be talking."

"I'd have known anyway, Finn. It's a *shanachie* I am, and haven't I told the story of Finn MacCool son of Cumal a hundred times or more. It's well I know the stories of the Fianna, that brave band of warriors of long ago."

"And are these stories popular?" Finn asks with a sheepish grin.

"Aye, but it's the women who most often ask to hear the sad tale of Sabd, and how you lost her to that wizard who lured her away when it was in the east you were fighting off the Northmen."

"Aye, it's more than a sad tale to me."

"If you don't mind my asking, Finn, it's a question I have that's always been on my mind. How is it you came to have the baby Oisin to raise as your son, when it was born in the wild he was?"

"How do you know of Oisin?"

"Aye, sure, but it's in the stories, just as surely as Oisin grows to be the greatest poet of all Ireland."

"But how can this be known?" asks Finn, bewildered and trying to shake off the blur of the poteen. "I've just come this day from finding my son in the forest where my hounds on the hunt came upon him in the wild. And sure I'm just after leaving him in the care of the Fenians, just a wee baby. He's no more a poet, than a blacksmith or a druid."

"It's all in the stories, man, and it's through the stories that beats the pulse of our people as well as the fate of Finn."

"So then what say the stories of the fate of Finn MacCool?"

"There's some say that you died, trying to quell an uprising among your own men, and others say that you fell asleep in a cave, waiting for such time as Ireland would need you again."

"Well, it's the second ending that suits me better." Finn lifts his glass to the mouth of the bottle that the old man tilts above it. "And more so if the call from that unborn generation is to defend the peace."

"Well, be sure to wake me from the dead because those times beyond the fear and misery that's on us, I'll want to see."

"It's whether I'm dead or alive right now, awake or dreaming, I can't tell, Owen Reilly."

"Well, if the question be drunk or sober, there's a question I can answer," says Reilly, breaking into a peal of laughter joined by Finn MacCool.

"And surely, Finn, you are alive, just as I am, because we're in the story now. Where but between the words of the tale do the shanakie and the hero come to life? Our soul dwells in the stories, Finn, and it's the stories that will keep us and our children Irish for all time."

"Then if it's no more than a story I am, how is it, Owen Reilly, that between us we've already downed half of this bottle of poteen?"

"If it is flesh and blood that you are, Finn, how is it you go riding with your hounds that never tire across forests long ago felled by the landlords?"

"How can you be telling me this, man, when it's just a day ago I was coming through the woods with the trees as wide as my horse is long?"

"Those were the ancient times, Finn, when the land and laws and all our ways were our own, and not the crooked maze of foreign minds in which we wander, starved and beaten, lost and dazed."

"So, what's to become of Ireland?"

"It's not a fortune teller I am, Finn. It's only old stories I have to tell, but it's one of them says that you'd be back to save her in her time of need."

Finn shakes his head, baffled by the words of Owen Reilly and the outcome of his own story. "My strength may be legendary, but a lone warrior's but a feeble man without his comrades by his side."

"It's the story, man, that'll save Ireland. It's the story that will bring the Fianna back to life and turn our minds back to who we truly are."

"You've much trust in tales, Owen Reilly."

"Aye, but haven't they been my stock and trade all my

life?"

"What of you, Owen Reilly? My head is muddled with trying to figure out my own. What's your story then?"

"It was as an old bachelor I was when I left Cavan after my own mother died, God rest her soul. What with no family of my own to keep me tethered to one place, I thought to travel the length and breadth of Ireland, working for wages and telling the stories of the ancient ones for a pint of ale or a plate of rashers. But hadn't I gotten half as far as Dublin when I came to Kildare and set eyes on my Maura. And there was an end to my traveling in the same year, nay, the same season that I had left home."

"What year was that?"

"Eighteen hundred and twenty-seven."

"Eighteen hundred and twenty-seven!" sputters Finn, spitting out his drink onto the flagstone floor. "My days in the saddle must've been years, and the months centuries! How is it so much time has passed?"

"Aye, but isn't that the way it is for us mortals as well. It's been two and twenty years since I wed my Maura here in this cottage, and still it feels like barely a day has passed. Yet the difference between those times and these is like poteen to water. What with the fiddlers playing and the fire roaring and a pig slaughtered to feed all who came to celebrate our *fheis*. Round the house and mind the dresser, such jigs and reels were danced as hadn't been seen since the fairies took to living under the hills."

"I've never been to a wedding," murmurs Svana from the corner where she feels like a leaf spinning in a stream as she listens, following the swirling currents of their stories.

"Have you not? Well, there's not been as lively a party in

all Ireland as we had that night in this cabin, not since the ancients held their feasts at Tara. And it was a happy life that followed. Mind we never had too much, but always enough and maybe a tad more for good measure."

"That's what Dagda always says."

"Aye, the Dagda, and his Cauldron of Undry, it's many a story I've told of him and the Dé Dannan. But, sure there's never a night long enough for telling all the tales."

"Then for now just tell us your own."

"Aye, my own with the best of it now over, a story no more or less real than the legends themselves."

"Did you have children?"

"Aye, three, and what with this tiny plot of earth giving enough *praties* to feed all five of us, they were good times. We raised a few pigs as well with one to pay the landlord once a year on *Gale Day* when his agent would come to collect the rent, and the rest for ourselves and some for any stranger who knocked on our door."

"It's the same hospitality has put a roof over the heads of the Fianna and kept us close to the heart of the people."

"I'm telling you, Finn, times have changed. What with the blight and the Red Coats coming soon after, many doors in Ireland have been bolted, and the misery of each household has become its own to keep."

"But why don't you hunt, man? What of the fields of grain that I saw with my own eyes waving to me as I rode in with the lass?"

"Surely, it's from ancient times you've been riding, Finn MacCool, not to know that an Irishman caught poaching on the acres that were once his own is a hunted man."

"Are you telling me it's a crime for a man to hunt and trap

his own land?"

"His own land is only what poor piece an Irishman can rent on the fringe of the estates of the landlords off living in England, the very place the grain'll go as soon as it's cut and bundled, with the Red Coats standing by to see it off at the dock. But what will come of us next year when we've no seed left to plant and no animals left to breed, is beyond any tale I've told."

"You know as well as I do, Owen Reilly, that our people are as versed in war as poetry. Why don't we fight?"

"Some have, with what strength they have left and what weapons they can forge. But what match is a pike or a pitchfork for the musket and ball of the Queen's soldiers."

"Musket and ball?"

"Ah, you've a fine store of words, Finn MaCool, but those are two you've yet to learn for it was with the spear and the blade that you fought. Well, how can I explain them? The musket and ball is like the sling and the stone, only the ball is shot with such force that it can kill a man far beyond the range of any *tathlum* slung by any Dé Dannan."

"So, you know of the tathlum?"

"Aye, the stories tell us of the sling-stone made of the blood of toads and bears and vipers mixed up with sea-sand and hardened. It was just such a stone as Lugh used to send Balor's eye sailing through his brain."

"The very same," says Finn draining the last drop of his drink.

"For all the force of the sling and tathlum, the musket and ball is deadlier still."

"If it's muskets they have, why haven't we the same?"

Outside the cottage they hear the clatter of hooves and the

muffled footfalls of bare feet on the hard ground. The old man stops talking and leans toward the door to listen. The hushed parade continues down the road and stops at the low wall surrounding the next yard.

"Sure, it's an education that you need, Finn MacCool, in the laws that have stripped our people bare to see how we've come to this poor place in time."

Rising from his place on the stool, he nods toward the door. "Come on then. It's time to get a lesson by the hedges on how it's come to be."

The Estate

Finn weaves across the boards of the cabin as he moves toward the door, but the commotion outside sobers him. Still groggy from the sip of poteen, Svana follows Owen Reilly to the front yard where they watch the crowd that has gathered just beyond the low wall of the next cottage draw back. Four men in red uniforms ride up to the gate behind the man who calls out.

"James Burke! We are here to take possession of this house."

"For pity's sake," Owen Reilly yells back at him. "Didn't Burke have a full beard on the day when I was born? Have you no mercy at all for a man older than your own grandfather, Dan Sheady."

"Silence, man! I'm here on the Queen's business."

"The Queen or the devil's?" yells a woman from the crowd.

"They're one in the same," cries another.

One of the soldiers fires his musket into the air. Svana flinches at its crack and fury.

"James Burke. We are here to take possession of this house."

A splinter of a voice pricks the silence that follows.

"Go back to hell where you came from!"

Sheady nods toward the cottage. Two of the soldiers dismount and ram their shoulders against the bolted door that bursts open as another climbs onto the roof, plucking off fistfuls of thatch that rain down on the ground.

The two soldiers come out of the cottage, carrying the old man, one bearing his skinny arms, the other his flailing legs and set him down cursing and screaming beneath the hedges along the side of the road.

"A curse on the devil who spat you from hell and all the generations to follow, you thieving bastards."

Sheady reaches for the coiled rope on the horn of his saddle and tosses it up to the soldier on the roof who attaches it to the main beam. He then dismounts to join the three others who leap to the ground, take hold of the rope and yank hard to take down the beam and with it the walls of the cottage.

Finn strides into the yard. The soldiers take no notice of the stranger who stands behind them in his shirt sleeves until he taps the broadest on the shoulder, landing a punch squarely on the jaw that has turned in his direction. A musket fires, more punches are thrown and in the mayhem that follows Finn's horse rears. Svana takes hold of its reins and mounts just as more red-coated soldiers come over the hill.

"We've a riot on our hands!" shouts a soldier from the roof.

"Beat them back," orders an officer before pounding the butt of his musket into the skull of the man who jabs his leg with a pitchfork, his horse trampling the body that crumples below its hooves. Then the bright flash of a musket precedes the cry of a woman whose boy falls by her side.

"Isn't it enough you've starved his brother?" the woman shrieks. The mother rocks the injured boy in her arms while the other women encircle her, their bodies thin as rails forming a stockade to protect the two while others run across the fields. Then from the flashing musket, the silver shadow of

Nuada's hand shoots out and flies past Svana's head where hovering above the haunches of Finn's horse, it draws open its fingers and smacks down hard. The rearing mare hits the ground and races across the field and over the hill with the cries and cracking muskets fading in the distance.

She hangs on tightly while miles upon miles of countryside, blurred by the mare's speed, fall away.

Tugging back on the reins, she tries to stop the horse that finally slows to a trot, coming to a halt where a crew of laborers wield picks and dig ditches, some carrying heavy stones. Another fifty workers sit huddled on the embankment, the smallest children among them, squatting closest to the wood fire into which they stare with empty eyes. Only one, a girl with matted hair and skinny arms that hang limply from the shift worn ragged by the wind and rain, turns her head to see the stranger. She rises and approaches Svana and tugs at the edge of her mantle.

"Have pity, miss," she whispers and points toward a *scalp*, the rough shelter dug into the embankment, lined with grass where a woman lies. Her wisps of sandy hair are stiff with mud. Her eyes flutter open.

"Money for food for the child," she feverishly mutters the words that she so often chants to passers-by. "Money for the child."

Svana dismounts and crosses to the woman's side. The little girl puts her head on her mother's stomach.

"I felt the baby move! I felt it!"

The mother runs her fingers through the girl's hay colored hair. "Did you now, love?"

Svana stands, baffled. What can she do? What could she have done for her own grandmother the night the banshee cried? She feels her own smallness, and it shames her. If she could pour what strength she has left and the health of her own body into this woman's, she would. A sharp crack rings off a boulder, startling her from her thoughts and to her feet. It is the whip of the overseer.

"Back to work or you're off the job. There's plenty ready to take your place," barks the man who towers above them, his stomach protruding over his belt, nodding toward the ragged crowd that sits by the side of the road.

"Whose horse?"

"My friend's."

"Your friend's? Then whose was it before he stole it?"

"He didn't steal it. It belongs to him."

"Oh, really, and you just borrowed it to take a little ride on the back roads. So, who's your friend?"

"Finn MacCool," Svana blurts out before she realizes how in this world that name belongs to a legend, and not to a living man.

"Oh, Finn MacCool, is it?"

"I mean it's my Uncle Finn's."

"So, your uncle's Finn MacCool, and my own father's Lugh of the Long Arm."

"He's just my cousin."

"Well, friend of Finn and cousin of Lugh, it's in jail you'll be with a noose around your neck soon to follow, for parading up and down these roads with a stolen horse."

"She's not stolen."

"And you're a liar, friend of Finn, and soon to be keeping company with the rats, leastwise till they hang you, horse thief that you are."

"Leave her alone, you bully."

"Shut up yourself, you slut."

"Don't you call my mother names!" shouts the little girl who takes up a stone and flings it at the overseer, hitting him squarely in the chest.

"Bridget, no!" cries the woman, pulling the child down to her side before the ganger can grab hold of her.

"Stop!" cries Svana as he raises his whip. "The horse is mine. What will you give me for her?"

He takes a greasy leather purse from his coat pocket. "It's a pound I'll give you to keep your mouth shut about wherever it was you took it from."

"A pound of what?" she asks, never having heard of such money in her time.

"So, it's a joker you are, is it? Well, there'll be nothing to laugh about if you should tell a living, breathing soul what you did with the horse." He hands her a crumpled bill. "Here, take it. Though you don't deserve more than a boot up the arse."

"You're a bully and a thief. It's her should be going for the Constable."

"Alright, I'll give her two, seeing as the saddle's a fine one. Now it's your mouths you'll keep shut, or it's off to jail with the lot of you."

She looks quizzically at the bills in her hand. "What good are these?"

"You could buy bread and a dress and even a doll," marvels the child staring at the bills. Svana hands the two pound notes to her.

"Ah, lass, sure but the hunger hasn't starved the kindness out of Ireland. It'll be enough to keep this one alive and bring the other into this world wailing. But unless it's a fairy that you are yourself, you'll be needing some for yourself." She takes one bill from her daughter and presses it back into the stranger's hand.

"Enough, now off with you!"

With another crack the whip wraps around her ankle, searing her flesh with a hot, stinging pain. "Damn you to hell," she shouts, and as he draws the whip back to strike again, Finn's horse rears, coming down hard and grazing the ganger's shoulder.

Stunned and bleeding on the ground, he lies there looking up with terror as the horse again rears. But before it comes down with its bone crushing force, Svana grabs its reins and yanks, deflecting the horse from the ganger's chest. Then as he shrugs off his daze, she mounts and gallops down the road.

She veers at a fork and turns down a narrow, pitted path. Riding on, she feels relieved to have only the company of the starlings that dart and weave in and out above the fields, that despite all the starvation she has witnessed, still wave with golden stalks. Approaching the next town, she finds more gruesome evidence that the food growing in the fields is not nourishing the bodies of those who planted it.

In the ditch lies a man, his knees drawn to its chest, his gaping mouth green with the leaves between his slack jaws. Svana thinks he is dead until he raises a bony hand in supplication, his jaws moving as he chews on the dandelions like a cow at its cud. Then further on by the side of the road is a woman with two children whose bellies are bloated with hunger, and in her arms she carries another, stiff and wrapped in a tattered shawl.

"Please, miss, have pity. Money for a poor babe's coffin."

She leans down from the horse to pass the pound note into

her hand.

"God bless you," she whispers.

Svana rides on. Ahead she sees another gang of workmen being harangued by an overseer with one eye that follows her suspiciously as she passes. She looks away from the other gaping hole that reminds her ominously of Balor. Giving the horse a light kick, she trots on faster, turning the head of any along the road who has strength enough to follow the roan steed's passage with weary eyes.

They do not stare at her, one more displaced person on the road, but at Finn's horse, its lustrous chestnut hide, flecked with tiny strokes of silver like frost on the autumn hillocks. She knows also that such attention might easily land her in jail with worse to follow. Soon after a carriage drawn by two dappled horses passes in which sits a finely dressed, but sickly looking man. No doubt, she thinks one of the gentry Owen Reilly spoke of, and boldly she rides up alongside him.

"Sir, my horse is a fine one, is she not?"

"Quite," drawls the man not without interest.

"My father bid me sell her for a fair price, what do you think that might be?"

"A farthing would be fair for the likes of you. But seeing as I am generous man, I'll give you ten pounds."

"Then she is yours."

"Follow me to the edge of my estate. There a boy will take it to the stable and you shall be paid."

She knows that she soon must eat and that the ten pounds will buy far more than the two she had been given by the ganger, but when they reach the gentleman's estate, a knot twists in her stomach when the stable boy opens the gate and the man in the carriage speaks to him. "See to the mare."

As he reaches for the horse's bridle, Svana holds tight to the reigns and pulls back.

"I'll take her now, miss. No need to worry, she'll be well cared for." He coaxes the reins from her hands, drawing her from the saddle. "I'll swear to that."

Standing by the mare, she sees herself reflected in the black globe of the horse's eye, a calm, dark world where if she could shrink herself to the size of a speck of dust, she would prefer to dwell on its inky surface than in any of the worlds through which the phantom winds have blown her.

"Here, take it." A five-pound note protrudes from between the man's thin white fingers, the tips manicured to petite crests. When she plucks it from between them, careful not to touch his skin, he grabs hold firmly of her wrist, regarding her intently with bloodshot eyes, embedded in the flabby folds and creases of his pale face.

When he speaks, she smells the foulness of his breath. "Not much meat on this chicken, but being young I'm sure it's tender."

A wave of revulsion radiates up her arm from the touch of his papery skin and the bony bracelet of his hand around her wrist. "Wait behind the stables after nightfall, and I will give you the rest and more," he says in a low voice before signaling to his liveried man to continue up the curving drive.

For a moment Svana stands stunned, sensible only to the creeping shame that inches over her. As she opens her hand a sudden breeze blows the five-pound note from her palm to the ground and sends it scuttling across the lawn, blowing away with it the sick feeling. The flight of the bill ends when the stable boy, who chases it across the grass, hurls himself down and sweeps it up just as she turns from the estate and hurries down the hedge lined path. Behind her she hears the padding of bare feet on the dirt road.

"Don't be daft," says the boy who approaches. He looks to be about her age, but his gray green eyes gaze at her with the assurance of one much older. "Sure, miss, he's black as a bog, but money's money. Just take it, and if you don't come back, there's no harm's done."

Svana turns to face him. "I'd scoop out the entrails of any animal five days dead before I'd touch gold from that foul hand."

The boy studies her with a mixture of disbelief and amusement. "Then it's poor you'll be your whole life surely, for any pence or pound that crosses your palm passed through his hand or one just like it."

"Then I'll starve."

"In these times, miss, that's no threat. It's the common lot to be sure."

She crosses her arms and stares at him. "I'll still not take it."

"Eammon!" an elderly man calls from the stable where he holds the bridle of Finn's mare, his own sparse tufts of hair as silver as the roan horse's mane. "Leave off flirting with the lass and get back to work!"

"Listen," he says tucking the five-pound note into the small pocket of the faded checkered vest he wears over a patched and tattered shirt. "Wait for me tonight at the dead oak on the edge of the field."

"Eammon O'Brien!"

"Ah, will you quiet down, Thomas, I'm coming." The boy reaches up and touches the sprig of berries still entangled in her hair that had been placed there by Holly. "You've got weeds growing out of your head, girl. Wait for me tonight and

I'll make sure that's it's a proper bed you have."

Svana watches the boy dart back toward the old man who scolds him for lingering, but with a shrug and a laugh, Eammon O'Brien takes hold of the horse and heads into the stable.

Without a destination of her own beyond sleep, Svana follows the boy's advice and crosses the open field through the tall grass glinting with the wild buds of yellow, blue and violet, marveling at their delicate, riotous beauty. How, she wonders, can nature still yield such loveliness in a world so violated, a world where the fruit is stolen from the very hands that plant and harvest it, the stewards of the earth who for their labors receive only scorn and starvation.

At the oak she settles herself inside the rotten hollow at the base of its trunk. Slanting rain rolls over the hill and splatters into her shelter. She slips off her mantle and hangs it over the gap to keep out the wet and windy blasts of air, and there in the dark and earthy womb, she curls up on the dried leaves and goes to sleep so deeply that she barely stirs when hours later the stable boy returns. He runs across the field and slipping her mantle from where it hangs, rolls and tucks it under his arm before hurrying back to the estate.

Scalpeen

Long past midnight lightening flares and curls like a fiery vine with one tendril whipping off a branch of the rotted oak. The limb cracks and falls with a crash and a rush of leaves. Svana stumbles out of the trunk drenched by the lashing rain. Wrapping her bare arms around herself, half-clad she circles the tree, searching for where the wind has tossed her cloak in the rain that tapers off to a drizzle.

With a rustling the tall grasses part, and a stooped and hooded figure appears crossing the field. She crawls back into the tree trunk, hoping she has not been seen. When she hears footsteps crushing the wet leaves, circling her hiding place, she stiffens and holds her breath.

The intruder stops at the base of the trunk, squats down and stares into the dark trunk. "Were you looking for this?" asks the stable boy with a grin, pulling the wet woolen mantel over his head.

"You took it?"

"Sorry, miss, but it was just to collect your money." His clenched hand enters the trunk and opens, revealing on his palm two five-pound notes. "He'd not have recognized you without it."

"What are you going on about?" she asks, crawling out from the gnarled lair.

"All I'm saying is that you're just after having a visit with your friend, Lord Kavendish. And it was with a blow to the head and a knee somewhat lower, that you impressed upon him the importance of paying money owed along with the respect that ought to be given to girls you do business with."

"You beat him?"

"Aye, roundly."

"Disguised as me?"

"Aye."

"You didn't kill him, did you? For if you've killed him, it's me they'll be after!"

"It was barely two taps that you gave him. And what with all the whiskey that was in him, he barely felt those. Just slipped to the ground in a heap, which is where you left him. Now c'mon. We've a long road ahead."

"And what makes you think I'd be going anywhere with the likes of you."

"You could have a bit more appreciation."

"Keep the money, I've no need of it."

"You're not going to start with the daft talk again, are you? But sure this time, you're right as rain for you'll have no use for it in jail."

"Do you think they'll be after me?"

"Well, we can stand here till dawn and see who comes up over the hillside to bid you good morning, or you can come with me someplace that they won't find us, where we can make ready to leave this mad place altogether."

Svana slips the mantle over her head and follows the stable boy through the tall grass across the fields. A few miles beyond the estate, they come to the edge of a bog where she stops on a mound from which a thin curl of smoke rises.

"Better step down from there."

"Why?" she asks when a sharp, angry voice emerges from underground.

"Jaysus, Mary and Joseph, get down off me bloody roof before I come and drag you off it myself!"

Perplexed, she takes hold of Eammon's outstretched hand and jumps to lower ground by his side. "Don't worry, lass," he chuckles. "It's not the fairies talking. Though Tessie's as little and belligerent as the worst of them."

Standing beside him, she can make out the contours of the sunken hut dug into the ground, thatched over with rushes and branches.

"Welcome to my *scalpeen.*"

"You live in the ground?"

"Whatever place you've tumbled from, you must have bumped your head badly if you don't remember that your own people have been driven down into the earth—that is those of us lucky enough to still be alive."

"Lucky! You call this lucky?" From a crawl space below her knees, juts out the tiny face of a creature that growls up at them between coughs.

"Tess, move aside and let us in."

"You nearly choked me out with that big lopper of a foot over the smoke hole. Now be gone with the both of you, for you're not coming in!"

"Is that as warm a welcome as you can conjure, Tess, for your own brother and a visitor in need of a bed?"

"I've had enough of your visitors, Eammon O'Brien. What with the last one coming here and shrieking, carrying on like you'd killed her prize calf."

"Oh, Bessie. Not to worry, she'll not be coming around

anymore."

"Why? Because you're sweet on someone new?"

"It's not that way."

"Well, whatever way it is, I'm not letting you in."

"Now, Tess, that's just plain rude."

"And you gone for three nights, leaving me to gnaw on a crust of bread. Then like the lord of the manor, you come stomping on the roof and expect me to put the kettle on for tea because you've decided to come home!"

"Stop your complaining, Tess, for I left you with enough oat cakes to choke a horse. Now out of the way, we're coming in."

Eammon crosses to the gouged-out doorway and drops to his knees.

The foxlike features of the tiny girl tighten as she glares at him and snarls before popping back into the dug-out, grumbling under her breath. Eammon crawls in behind her, and Svana follows.

Inside the scalpeen she marvels at the snugness of the shelter—dug into the earth so no wind can penetrate with a small peat fire to warm the cozy den. There are two pallets of sewn animal hides stuffed with straw and a tree stump table flanked by two stools.

Standing over the small wooden table Eammon unknots the bulging napkin that hangs from the length of rope he wears to hold his tattered trousers suspended over his narrow hips. He pulls back the grimy linen folds to display the roasted meat of a wild bird. As he turns to reach for the cracked plates and bent cutlery from the rough-hewn shelf behind him, Tess leaps from her place, snatches up the crispy carcass and falls upon it like a half-starved cub.

"Tess, was it raised in the woods with wild creatures you were?"

Her cheeks bulge as she chews noisily. "It's only since we moved to this cave that I've had to take on their ways."

He crosses to where she squats on the floor and skewers the bird with his pocket knife, placing it on a tin plate. "If not for this cave that Tomas and I dug with our own picks and shovels, we'd be two more phantoms begging on the roadside."

Licking her palms and sucking her fingertips Tess glowers at him while he carves the poultry, before turning her sullen gaze on the stranger. "It's meant for me."

"It's meant to share," says Eammon, doling out two equal portions and placing them on opposite sides of the stump. "If I were you, miss, I'd bolt that down without so much as saying grace, for it's a crafty little animal she is, and she'll have swallowed your last bite before you've so much as said amen."

Tess snarls again and crosses to the table where Svana delicately braces the breast of the bird between two ribs with her knife while tearing strands of meat from the bone with her fingertips from which she eats hungrily.

She stares at the guest who looks first at the meat in her hand and then back at Tess. "And why is it you scold me for bad manners, but you'll not say a word to her?"

"I've not done anything wrong, have I?"

Tess lifts the fork from beside her own plate and raises a morsel to her lips. "It's called a fork."

"How very useful," exclaims Svana, never having used such a utensil. "Here I was thinking it was an odd sort of comb."

"And have you never seen a fork before?"

"No, are they very common in this province?"

"About as common as the lunatic girls my brother does be bringing home."

"Tess, even if once I saw you eating properly the way Mammy taught you, you've no right to talk to others that way. And she's only the second visitor I've brought here."

"Aye, and the one dafter than the other."

"Aren't you hungry yourself?" Svana asks Eammon, awkwardly maneuvering a chunk of meat to her lips with the fork.

"Thanks, but I've already eaten."

"So, Bessie is still slipping you tasty morsels out the backdoor of his Lordship's kitchen."

"I told you already, Tess, it's done with her I am. She's nothing but bossiness and trouble, and sure don't I have my share of both with you."

Tess nods and smiles broadly. "Aye, that you do." A shadow of suspicion crosses her wrinkled brow. "But if you've already had your supper, and it wasn't stolen by Bess from his Lordship's table then, Eammon, you've been at it again."

"At what?"

"Poaching."

"Poaching," he spits the word back at her like a bitter seed. "Is it poaching when you set your nets and snares on the very acres stolen out from under you?"

"It's to the Magistrate you can ask that question, Eammon, before he sends you off to Botany Bay."

"Botany Bay, is that far from here?"

Tess rolls her eyes in disbelief at the stranger's ignorance.

"Was it dropped on your head you were at birth, girl, or have you just gone mad with the hunger?"

"I'll not deny I've been turned around ever since I was forced from my own home."

"So, you see, Tess, it's evicted she's been just like ourselves. But how is it that you've not heard of that hell on earth where decent Irish men and women are deported, condemned to be worked to death for the crime of trying to feed their own families and keep a roof over their heads?"

"It's to a prison they sent my Dah away to a land far to the south they call Australia."

"And it's the same long way that we'll be traveling soon enough."

"Eammon, now it's you who does be talking daft. How could we ever pay for passage when we haven't so much as a penny to buy a pinch of tea?" Tucking two fingers into the narrow pocket of his worn vest, he fishes out the two five pound notes. "Ten pounds?" she whimpers. "For that they'll hang you surely."

"Oh, Tessie, will you give it a rest before you bring us worse luck with all your worry. Ten pounds, Tess, there's enough to pay our passage out of Ireland and all the misery that's in it."

He glances toward Svana. "That is if you'll come with us."

"My way is not my own, though even if it were, I'd not leave Ireland for it's hope I still have of finding my own family."

"Eammon, have you lost your wits completely, taking up with a gypsy girl whose thieving ways will only take you to the gallows."

"Tess, the money's not stolen. It's her that Lord Kavendish

robbed, paying ten pounds for a mare worth five times that and more, and just to get that paltry payment it took a few hard blows to make an honest man of him."

"Surely, Eammon, boys hang for less."

"Will you calm yourself, Tessie? Nobody's going to be hung for it would take the cry of the banshees themselves to wake his Lordship from his drunken stupor. Even then the drunk old sot's not likely to remember what happened tonight for it was a full jug of poteen I brought him and a full jug that he guzzled down. Why, it was enough whiskey to erase the memory of all Ireland."

"But what if he does, Eammon? What if someone else saw you? Surely he'll call for the Constable."

"If Fer Leath himself came looking for us out on the edge of this bog, he'd not find our scalpeen."

"Are y'sure, Eammon?"

"Aye, lass, I'm sure."

Tess' face brightens. "So, you really whacked him then, Eammon?"

"Aye, what with the whiskey that was in him, the one blow to the head and the other somewhat lower, he slunk to the ground like a slug."

"Ah, Eammon, I wish I'd have been there."

"Lucky for him that you weren't," he says with a wink toward Svana. "For Tess is a scrappy one. She'd have torn his bloated face right off the bone."

Tess glows with pride at the compliment. "Then I'd have twisted his wicked skull right off his wicked shoulders and thrown it into the briars the way I should have done the day they came for Dah."

"Tess, you were barely old enough to tie your own boot

BOOK THREE

laces, you can't go blaming yourself."

"What happened?"

"The soldiers took him," Tess utters with contempt, digging her cracked and dirty nails into the palm of her hand

"Aye. They took him."

A damp chill settles around them while in the silence her sadness fills the scalpeen. Tess crosses over to her pallet by the wall, drawing her knees to her chest. She holds the corner of a worn blanket to her cheek, places her thumb in her mouth and rests a finger across the bridge of her nose.

"They want it all. They twist the laws to steal the land, and mark me, they'll steal the water from the well before they're through. When the first harvest of praties turned black in the field, an oozing mush that ran through our fingers and our last pig gone to pay the rent on Gale Day, Dah took to setting his traps on the ridge at the edge of the estate. We knew Lord Kavendish was intent on clearing the land of tenants to make way for pasture and that he'd use the law to do it if we gave him half a chance, but it was only by poaching he could feed us."

"For that they took him?"

"That and what followed. For first the Constable came, but being a coward he waited till Dah and I were out on the bog cutting turf to come nosing around our cabin. But my mother was a feisty one when the anger was on her, and his questions were met with only curses and his grab for the pot where two hares were stewing earned him a hot poker across his thieving hands."

"Mamó would have done the same."

"The next day he came with three soldiers and Lord Kavendish himself. But my dah was ready for them with his pike sharpened, and like a Fenian of old he fought, but one man is no match for cowards with pistols, and they took him away in irons."

"And sent him then to Botany Bay?"

"First to Dublin to sit out the winter in that dank, cold cell to await a trial that the Magistrate rushed through with an eye on his pocket watch and his mind on his dinner. Sentencing my father to deportation and my mother wrecked with the misery of it all."

Svana shakes her head sadly. "Will you find him do you think?"

"If there's a ship sailing out of Ireland, I'd be a poor excuse of a son not to try."

Tess sits up and chatters away fretfully.

"But who's to say Dah will be there when we get there, and who's to say it won't be worse than here? At least here we've our own place, and I'm safe from all the strange things that might happen on the deck of some leaky ship tossing about on the waves. And what if you fall off, have you thought of that I wonder, Eammon? Who'd care for me then, I'd like to know? And what of the serpents? I've heard there are monsters with jaws that swallow ships whole, and that's after they've bounced them around on their tails to break them up so they're easier going down. Have you thought of any of that now I wonder, you with your grand plan?"

"Tessie, it's here in Ireland the serpents dwell. Haven't we seen them ourselves, breaking up the land and devouring the acres along with the families that tilled them? It's across the sea we'll escape them. So don't go stirring yourself up over all the fearful things that might happen when it's far worse we've already had done to us."

"But, Eammon, I'm afraid."

"To stay here is to die surely, Tess. Can't you see we've no choice but to leave and start again some place new?"

"I'll not go."

"That you will. Even if I have to wrap you up in that blanket and carry you onto the ship and stow you under my bunk until we're out at sea."

"But I don't want to go."

"I don't want to leave Ireland any more than you do, Tess, but that's just the way it's going to be. So settle yourself down and I'll play you a tune."

From the pine shelf he takes his tin whistle and plays the same ballad that Svana's grandmother sang to her that night before the banshees cried. She hums along softly with the sliding notes that soothe the restless child who closes her eyes and drifts off to sleep. With the notes of that ancient melody she can almost feel the tug of her grandmother's fingers twisting her hair into braids, and with the memory washing over her a wave of sadness.

After the last gliding note dissolves in the air between them, Eammon nods toward his straw-filled mat. "You look done in, lass. Lie down and take your rest. It was a rough night you had of it out there in that storm."

"Sure, but it's been more than one night I've slept on the windward side of the hills," she says, crossing to his bed. "But where will you sleep?"

"I'm like my father when the mood is on me. I remember how he'd put us to sleep with a ballad and play through the night, waking us up in the morning with a reel or a jig. Sure, but he could have the devil himself up and dancing at dawn, my mother used to say."

Eammon glances up to see his strange visitor has already dozed off, the slight, disheveled girl whose appearance has already shifted the direction of his life. And as he plays all the airs his father taught him, even the most mournful is tinged with hope. All through the night the music of his tin whistle fills the scalpeen until a single strand of salmon light streams across the crawl space and trickles along the earthen floor.

Finally he tucks his instrument into the long satin pocket that his mother had sewn into the lining of his vest. Then taking a knife from the table, he kneels by the ring of stones that encircles the still smoldering sods and pries up a flat blue-gray stone. From a shallow hole in the damp earth he removes a wooden box and pulls back the lid on its rusted hinges to lift out a tattered bit of purple cloth bound with a green silk thread. Carefully he unweaves the thin bindings and opens the battered bit of cloth and removes from its folds a strand of shellacked beads: ten sets of ten each separated by a knot in the leather strand.

"Eammon, what's that you've got there?" Tess is leaning over her brother's shoulder sleepily.

"Jaysus, girl, don't go sneaking up on me like that."

"I wasn't sneaking, I'm just up. Those were Mammy's, right?"

"Yes, Dah made them for her."

"I remember she held them a lot."

"Every night she'd set a prayer on each bead, and sometimes when she'd said them all, she'd start again."

"I miss Mammy."

"And I know that's why you don't want to leave this place, but Mammy would want us to go."

"But once we leave here, maybe I won't remember, and

maybe she won't remember me. Maybe if I'm not here, she'll look down from heaven and think I ran away and not know where to find me. And then maybe she'll forget me altogether."

Eammon places the rosary of dried seeds worn thin from the gentle grip of their mother's fingertips around his little sister's neck. "Wear these, and she'll be able to find us. And every time you say your prayers the way she taught us, she'll smile. Trust me, she wants us to go, and it's her that will keep us safe."

"Do you really think so?"

"Aye, lass, I'm sure of it."

Tess hugs her brother, holding him tightly until she notices the open box and nearly shoves him off the stool to get to it. "What else have you got hid away in there?"

"There's nothing else," he says, trying to grab it back from her tight grip.

"I just want to see."

"Careful with it, Tess. It's very old."

The child pulls back the folded bit of fabric, and her eyes widen at the sight of the blue stone set in the silver brooch. "Whose pocket did you pinch this from?"

"Tess, it's ours. Mammy left it for us, but she told me not to show it to you until you were old enough not to go telling our business for fear that a thief would come and take it from us."

"The stone's so pretty. It's like a lake, a fairy lake," marvels Tess, staring into the hazy blue gem at its center. "Where'd Mammy get it?"

"Her mammy, and she got it from her mammy before her. She said it came from a time so long ago it was nearly past remembering. She said I should keep it safe for you until you would know better than to tell anyone or lose it."

"I won't tell anyone, I swear."

Startled they both turn to see the stranger behind them stir in bed. "Hide it. I don't trust her," whispers Tess, hastily handing the brooch to Eammon who pins the tarnished silver disk inside the lining of his vest for safe keeping on their journey.

"Now put the kettle on. I've some nettles and honey for tea, and soon we'll be heading off." The sleepy child nods and fills the battered kettle with water from the clay pitcher, setting it over the fire as Svana sits up and stretches lazily.

"You were spying, weren't you?"

"Tess, for the hundredth time speak with a civil tongue."

"So, what's your name anyway?"

"Svanhildur."

"How is it that your mammy stuck you with such a silly name?"

"Mind your manners, girl, or go out into the field to grunt and nag at your wild cousins. For its convinced I am that somehow their blood is mingled with your own."

"But, Eammon, her mother must have been as daft as she is to come up with such a silly name."

"Enough, Tess."

"It's alright. I don't remember her very well, just her voice which was lovely. She died when I was very young."

"My mammy died too. I'm sorry about what I said, it's not so bad a name."

"You can call me Svana."

"I was beginning to wonder if you had a name at all, or where it was you came from."

"From where do you think I've come?"

"The west, for the west is where my mother said the magic still resides."

"Is there no magic here?"

"Look around, lass, and tell me that yourself. What with drunken landlords and families being evicted to live as bog squatters, what magic do you see here? Though I've heard that they've had their share of hardship to the west as well."

Tess' eyes brighten. "But it's there atop Knocknarea that Queen Maeve still sits, and on the shore of Lough Arrow that the ancient ones still battle."

At the mention of the places she so recently visited, Svana pales. "How is it, Tess, that you know all this if you've not seen it for yourself?"

"Some of them come to me in dreams, but mostly though I heard from my mammy."

"How is it your mother came to know the old stories?"

"It wasn't here that she was born, but in County Sligo. In that place by the sea that her own mother had heard the tales told by her own grandmother, and so the tales were said to go all the way back to the one who had learned them herself from the very gods and warriors who resided in them."

As if an arrow just whizzed by her ear, Svana sits stunned. Clearly, she has returned to the land of the living, but somehow she herself has become part of the legends of its distant past. She knows no words can convey to Eammon that she is in fact that ancestor without appearing mad.

"So then," she falters. "It's from the west that you think I am?"

"Aye, and not from any place above the ground, for there's something unearthly strange about you surely."

"So, am I a fairy?"

"Aye, that would be my guess. A daughter of that ancient tribe, driven below the earth where the restless spirits dwell year-round, except on the eve of Samhain when the gates of your realm open and you walk the fields freely, waiting for some poor mortal unfortunate enough to cross your path to stumble in."

"Perhaps then, I am that poor mortal. Perhaps it was I who they took as a plaything to toss about from age to age to wander in the fields from which they'd been driven."

"Take me back, take me back."

"To meet the ancient ones?"

"No, to steal the great pot of Dagda, the Cauldron of Undry, so that I could eat my fill, then bring it back and feed all the hungry people."

"I've wished that myself."

"It's all just stories, Tess. Gods and their magical pots and weapons. I've heard it all, but I believe none of it."

"What if I were to tell you then that I met them. Lugh, Dagda, and his daughter Bridey? What if I told you that they were my friends?"

"Fine friends, I'd say, who leave you to wander in these hard times without food or a weapon." Eammon crosses to the entranceway of the scalpeen at the sound of approaching hooves. "Strange, no one rides out this way."

Tess has already scooted under the purple blanket on her mattress where she cowers. "I'm scared."

"It's only Thomas," says Eammon crawling outside onto the misty bog followed by Svana who recognizes Finn's roan mare and the old man who rides her, whose tufts of white hair stand out like the quills of an agitated hedgehog. Squinting to adjust to the daylight, she faintly sees the silver outline of the hand fluttering and rising on a flume of smoke, reminding her that although their quest has led her to a distant age that she must continue toward Tara.

"You're in danger," he warns. "A ganger arrived at first light with the Constable and made inquiries about the roan mare."

"Did you speak to them?"

"No, I was just coming out of the stable. Bess got to them first."

"Ah, no, not Bess."

"When I came up to them she was in the middle of telling them how she'd heard you scheming with the girl to run off together."

"Bessie and her lies." Eammon shakes his head with disgust.

"A woman scorned is bound to be a danger. She said she saw you riding off on the roan mare."

"But didn't they see the horse was still in its stall?"

"You know his Lordship. He'd make sure you were hung for plotting to steal the mare as surely as if you'd taken it, so I led the roan mare out through the orchard and rode her here," he says dismounting. "If it's hung as a horse thief you'll be, you might as well have the horse." Thomas hands the reins to Eammon as Svana strokes the horse's muzzle, glad to be back in her company though frightened at the thought of those in pursuit.

"Stay off the high-road and take the *boreens*. They're slower to travel, but you'll be safe in the hills. Is your plan still to board a ship out of Dublin?"

"Aye, it seems the surest way out."

"Then I'll head back and tell them that it's to Cork you

meant to travel, so you'll be safe heading east."

Eammon sets Tess in the saddle as the old man reaches up and places his leathery hand over the boy's.

"God be with you."

"And with you, Thomas Lynch. Whether it's in this world or the next may fair winds and good fortune bring us together again."

"Aye, let's hope so, lad." Thomas heads off in the direction of the estate while Finn's roan mare trots down the narrow cow path toward the hills.

Bounty

The birds of the orchard twitter and trill, darting from tree to tree, dipping and diving above the fields that surround the manor house. But their song does not distract the young woman in the starched white cap and apron who crosses from the back-kitchen door to the byre from her own mutterings. "Thinks he can toss me aside for a dirty little gypsy girl, does he?"

Bess becomes silent at the sight of the two men who arrived to the estate at dawn, stepping out of the kitchen where they have just eaten their fill of rashers, eggs and toasted soda bread. One is a portly man who tightly grips a coiled whip in his hand, and the other a scarecrow dressed in the uniform of the Constabulary, his tall blue hat too big for his narrow brow held on by a leather strap under the chin. The other is the ganger who carries his coiled whip by his side.

"Thank you, lass, in the name of the Royal Irish Constabulary," says the scrawnier of the two, lightly touching the brim of his ill-fitting hat.

Bess blushes at the attention that only inspires her to warble away happily with more lies. "Now remember, sir, he's dangerous when the anger is on him. Why his own father was sent away for nearly killing five men unprovoked. And the gypsy girl's a bad one too, and the child's not t'be trifled with either."

"C'mon," says the ganger gruffly. "We've no time for her."

"Aye, for it's the Queen's business we're on," adds the Constable importantly, beaming at Bess who beams back at him as the two men cross the yard toward their own sagging mares.

"God's speed," Bess calls, but her smile abruptly fades when taking a step back her bare foot brushes the leather of a boot in the doorway of the stable where, bloody and bruised, the sprawled body of Lord Kavendish lies lifeless. Like a banshee arrived late over the corpse, Bess stands screeching over the filthy body, but when it rolls on its side and groans, she screams even louder.

"Shut it, woman, with your ghastly wailing," drawls Lord Kavendish. The Constable hurries to the scene, placing his arm around her shoulder, the sleeve of his tight jacket rising nearly to his elbow.

"I thought it was a dead man waking."

"There, there, girleen, calm yourself now."

"Forget the girl, you ninny, and let's get his Lordship off the ground."

Each man takes a limp limb and lifts the whiskey-numbed body onto a nearby milking stool where it teeters perilously to the left, and when they sit it upright again, it leans even more perilously to the right.

"What's the time?" Kavendish mutters, fishing a gold watch the size of a plum from the pocket of his soiled brocade vest. He snaps it open and regards its face with disdain. "Damn these contrivances," he snarls, letting it drop and dangle from its white gold fob.

BOOK THREE

He squints at the Constable and ganger, trying to discern their number from the blurry group before him. "Did I summon the Constabulary?" he slurs, and then trying to focus on the ganger. "And who are these filthy rogues?"

"It seems, your Excellency," stammers the Constable. "There's been a theft."

"Theft," mumbles the landlord. "Not a day that passes that these filthy farmers don't rob me blind with their pathetic excuses instead of rent. Nearly ruined me."

From the waist he leans forward until his pointy chin rests on his knees and his arms, fringed with tattered lace, dangling by side.

"Actually, your Lordship, the mare was stolen."

"What mare?" Kavendish sits up, the news sobering him.

"The roan steed you purchased from the gypsy girl."

"What?" roars the landlord. "Bring me the stable boy. I'll whip the skin off his bone!" Losing his balance, he quickly seats himself again.

"Actually, your Lordship, the boy stole the horse."

"And the gypsy girl," chimes in Bess. "She put him up to it."

The veins beneath his temples swell, and his bleary eyes set in thick pouches of flesh narrow. "She shall hang by his side."

The ganger steps forward, nervously running his thumb along the handle of his whip. "What the Constable hasn't told you, sir, is how the girl came to have the horse. That is, if I may make bold to tell you, sir, how she came to have my horse."

"What are you babbling about, man? I'll have none of your meandering tales."

"The mare, sir, she's mine. Twenty pounds I paid the conniving gypsy for her."

"How dare you speak to me of ownership," snarls Kavendish, his words no longer slurred, the anger clearing his vision. "Unless you have proper documents to support your claim, remove yourself from my estate before I have you arrested as well."

"But, your Lordship, I paid twenty pounds."

"And I'll pay you double that for the mare's return and double again for that thief."

With a wink and a nod the ganger and Constable make their pact. "Aye, that we will."

The drunkard struggles to his feet and veers to his left until hitting a beam that bolsters up his sagging body.

"Is it to the manor house you'd like us to take you, sir?"

"I'd sooner let the pigs in the parlor than allow your dung covered boots on my carpets."

With that he draws a red silk handkerchief from his sleeve, dabbing his thin, chalky lips daintily before doubling over and retching up the remains of his previous night's excesses. Then drawing himself up proudly, he bobs and sways toward the mansion.

"Wait!" Bess hurries toward the men as they mount their horses. "Let me go with you. I know where the thief would have taken her. Nobody but me knows the place he dug his lair."

"We've no time to waste on the girl."

"As an officer of Royal Irish Constabulary…"

"Then bring the girl if you must, just shut your gob."

Bess smiles radiantly, raising her calloused barefoot into the stirrup and her plump rear onto the saddle with the

Constable's eager assistance.

Thomas appears running down the long drive toward the yard.

"Wait!" he calls, opening the gate and hurrying toward them. "I'm just after seeing them ride full kilter down the road. It's south they're headed toward Cork."

"Don't believe a word of it. It's like a father he is to the boy," shouts Bess as the Constable stretches his spindly arms around her waist to grab hold of the reins. "I'll take you to him."

"Bess, it's no match I am for your wits," replies Thomas with a shrug, standing before them breathless from the miles he has run for just such a chance to derail the chase before it begins. "Indeed, it was there on the bog I left him. And since there's no fooling you, Bess. It's from Waterford they plan to sail."

"No doubt that filthy gypsy was with him."

"Aye, I can't lie to you, Bessie. That she was."

The Constable nods toward Thomas.

"As an officer of the Royal Irish Constabulary…"

"There's money to be had, man, but I'll not be a pound richer standing here and listening to your blather." The ganger puts his spurs to his horse's side and gallops out of the yard followed by Bess and her officer in the direction of the bog.

Return of Brann

Steering clear of the high-road, Eammon leads Finn's mare along the boreens that crisscross the estate until the brambles grow too thick to pass, and they veer toward a pond where under the cover of a willow tree they stop to rest.

"I'm hungry," whimpers Tess.

"Tess, we have to keep moving."

"You said banshees couldn't wake up Lord Kavendish, and if it's the Constable you're worried about Thomas will take care of him with his story of us going to Cork."

"Well, I'm glad your hunger has cured your worrisome nature, but unless we're to eat the five-pound notes in my pocket, I've nothing to feed you."

"Ah, but this pond has plenty." Svana pulls open the green silk purse that dangles from her waist. From it she takes the gorge her father carved from the badger bone by the shore of Lough Arrow. Then into the murky water, she lowers the jagged bone on its silken line.

Barely has it sunk past the surface when the line tautens and with one swift movement, Svana tosses a silvery trout onto the shore. Tess chases and lunges at the flapping fish until Eammon grabs it by its tail and with both hands bashes its head on a stone. Dislodging the gorge, he flings it back to

Svana who angles for another as Tess scrambles up into the branches of a nearby aspen tree, its small leave chattering in the breeze.

Higher and higher she climbs until out pops her head with its mass of mouse brown curls silhouetted against the clouds.

"Tess, come down out of there," calls Eammon as he scales and guts the fish.

"I'm up too high. Can't hear you," she lies, climbing to an even loftier branch.

When into the tall grass Svana tosses a shimmering perch, Eammon looks on in amazement. "Is it by the magic of some fairy incantation that you lure them from beneath the rocks?"

"My father was a Northman. Grand fishermen they are in the north." She crosses to where he pinches open the sides of the mouth of a perch to remove the gorge.

"I see, so that makes you not an Irish maid at all, but a Viking."

"Some say so."

"How many other tales can you conjure with those lips?"

"Many," she responds, startled by the quick kiss, a kiss intended for her mouth, but that lands on her ear when at the crucial moment she turns her cheek.

A derisive shriek rises from the branches above them. "Eammon's got a sweetheart. Eammon's got," Tess taunts until with a crack, crack, crack and a rustle of leaves, she falls into a clump of thorny bushes by the bank.

"Tess!" cries Svana, hurrying to where the child lies motionless, her arms and legs entangled in the branches. Carefully they pull each aside, lift and lie her down on the grassy bank.

"Tess, are you alright there, girl?"

A spray of spittle splatters his face as the child breaks into a fit of renewed laughter.

"Eammon's got a sweetheart."

"Quiet down or it's to the top I'll carry you and drop you myself." Her giggles turn into a whimper and a groan as she holds a bloody hand over her swollen eye.

"I know a plant that grows on the bank of the stream. My grandmother used to peel back its leaves and press its balm onto the cut."

Tess groans again. "So, don't stand there like a cow, go and get some."

"Tess, don't be so bossy."

"And you stay here and play me a tune," she orders rolling on her side and popping her thumb into her mouth.

He seats himself beside her and takes his tin whistle from his vest pocket. "The pharaohs of Egypt weren't half the tyrant you are."

The lilting notes he plays seem to glisten on the leaves and skim the shimmering water like long legged silver insects. Along the edge of the stream Svana hunts for the succulent, thick leafed plant as the music fades into the sound of the water splashing over the rocks. Then in the muddy soil, she finds a clump of the pale green plant, and kneeling beside it, plucks its plump leaves into her cupped hand.

The current running over the pebbles seems to chatter with an invitation to step over them into the cool running water. Then there is a rustling nearby. Svana crouches and peers up through the bushes, watching Eammon approach.

She picks a hard red berry from a nearby bush and flicks it at him. As he looks about bewildered, she launches another hitting him on the brow. Quick as the perch that Svana had flung from the water, he is beside her. Losing her footing, she falls against him, and they topple into the spring where they sit for a moment in the cool water with the boat-like leaves that fall from her hand bobbing and racing downstream.

"So, is it to the Other Side you're taking me?"

"Is that where you're convinced I'm from?"

"I know how it is with you fairies. Under the water and through your magical portal."

"If I am a fairy, aren't you afraid I'll take a foolish mortal like you with me."

Eammon doesn't answer. Instead his face loses its teasing look, and tilting his head, he leans in closer toward her. She slips back, surprised by his sudden movement, and then briefly, only as long as his lips rest on hers, she feels a new sensation—a wave of calm and pleasure that for a moment makes her feel well placed, not lost, not alone, not pursued, not bewildered, but whole and happy.

"Aren't you ashamed of yourselves," scolds Tess from the shore, leaving a small child alone with bears and wizards and who knows what form of dangerous creature roaming these hills?"

"Not to worry. No claws would be a match for yours, it's often enough I've been scratched and gouged by them. And no wizard could stand still long enough to cast a spell what with you nagging at him with that sharp tongue of yours."

"Aye," agrees Tess proudly, patting the muzzle of Finn's chestnut mare whose flecks of silver gleam in the light reflected off the water.

"But still you shouldn't run off like that," the child whines. Then wincing with a sudden pain, raises a hand to where a welt has risen over her eye.

Eammon takes the linen cloth from his belt, dips it in the cool water, wrings it out and crosses to her, placing it gently across her brow.

"Sure, but you're more a danger to yourself than any demon you can dream up."

"I'm tired. I want my blanket."

When he raises his little sister from the ground, she tucks her cheek below his shoulder and sucks on her thumb intently.

The two disappear over the rise toward the willow tree as Svana sits in the cool running water, glad after all the centuries she has traveled to have a quiet bath. Wriggling out of the drenched mantle, she tightly twists its dusty folds, beating it on a boulder. She rinses it until the water runs clear, spreading it out over a bush to dry. A breeze touches her bare skin as she wades out beyond the pebbles.

She likes the feel of her feet sinking into the silky wet sand. Inch by inch she ventures out, the water deepening, rising up her sturdy calves and thighs to her waist, her ecru shift floating about her like a lily pad. The coolness of the water soothes her road weary muscles, and the shifting currents ease away the stress of worry and all the memory of her hard travels.

Halfway out into the pond, the soft babble of the stream that feeds it tempts her to take another step, then another — up to her ribs, her breasts and now her shoulders. There she stands, facing upstream, her hands stretching forward. When she begins to push away the water as it rushes past her, the current carries her legs upward, and there on her stomach with her chin still in the water, she floats and for the first time swims.

She has heard of men swimming. Northmen and fishermen, but never did she imagine the pleasure of her hands darting forward and returning to her sides, darting forward and returning to her sides as her feet gently kick, and her body rides along as if a hundred fairy hands are holding her aloft.

Her mind becomes clear. In all this topsy-turvy coming and going from one world to the next, time is no more than an element that like this stream carries her along and spins her about like the tiny leaves that bob and race along its surface. Svana realizes that if she stays calm, she can float and maneuver without harm, and that letting go of the weight of fear, she can enjoy the movement of nature on the currents of time.

Her calm and concentration are broken by the crackling of branches on the far side of the stream. Moving down the slope toward the shore, she sees the broad figure of a man approaching.

"The ganger," she thinks, taking a frightened breath and with it a gulp of gray water. She spits it out and chokes, flailing her tense arms while crying out to warn Eammon and Tess of the danger. But her cry is garbled and her view of the shore is blurred by the water between her and the air.

The more she struggles to rise, the more desperately her feet kick downward, trying to find level ground. Deeper and deeper she sinks, the sky growing dark with the shadows of the pond. Finally her body stops struggling and she sees her own fear rising in the pocket of air from her last exhalation. And in that white globe spiraling to the surface, she sees her grandmother laboring in the vegetable patch behind their dome shaped house.

Beyond fear or hope, Svana watches the image of her home

float above her, and just as it pops, she sees four massive, bristly legs thrashing down into the water.

A jaw surrounds her narrow arm, but with only enough force to pull her upward without breaking the skin, the beast draws her to the surface where two callused hands reach out for her. She coughs and sputters as the bristly wolfhound barks loudly, and his master carries her onto the grassy bank.

"That's the second time Brann's saved you."

Finn sets her down by a boulder where she wipes the water from her eyes that blurs the image of her friends. Panting, Brann sits by her side, and with his rough tongue licks her dripping face from chin to brow.

"Aye, Finn, it's good to see you both."

"From the looks of it, lassie, a minute more and it's to Tirnanóg you'd have been paying a visit."

"Mamó told me of that place. Do you know how to get there?"

"Some say it's reached through wells and ponds, a place like no other where there is nothing save truth and abundance, where there is neither age, nor decay, nor sadness."

"Have you been there, Finn?"

"Tirnanóg wouldn't be for the likes of me. Though food there is said to be good and plentiful, it's too fond I am of the hunt, and it's the company of my own lads around a smoldering pit of roasting meat I prefer to the lavish feasts of fairy land. One Fenian found his way there and when asked how he liked it replied that he'd rather be the lowest servant of the Fianna than a prince of Tirnanóg. Besides I'm not sure they'd let Brann in with me. And it's nowhere I'd be going without him." Finn's massive gray wolf hound sits by his side,

BOOK THREE

the corners of his mouth curling in a grin.

"Aye," says Svana hugging his neck gratefully. "He's a grand dog."

"There may be dogs as good as Brann, but none better."

"And have you found Sabd or the Fianna?"

"It's been no one I've seen but the red-coated devils and their henchmen who slapped the irons on me. Then for two nights I sat on a plank board behind bars in their rank jail. But on the morning the guard slipped a tin of gray gruel to me, I grabbed the blackguard's head through the bars and gave him a good battering until his Irish sense returned, and it was the key he handed me." Finn pours the water from his boots. "And what of you, lassie? Have you found your father?"

"No, but I met a boy. His name's Eammon O'Brien and he has a little sister Tess, and it's so bad for them that they're set on leaving Ireland altogether."

"It's hard times that be on us when the children are driven from their home."

"They were on their way to Dublin but didn't get far when Tess fell from an awful height. They're just over that rise under the willow. Why don't you go and check on the girl while I gather some leaves for her cuts and scratches?"

Finn tugs on his boots. "Aye, lassie."

"Don't mention that you're Finn MacCool. Eammon doesn't believe in the stories. Just tell them that you're my Uncle Finn."

"Why there's no lie in that, for to every Irish lass and lad it's like an uncle I am," he replies as he climbs the low rise toward where Tess sits with her knees drawn to her chest, staring angrily into the fire through her one eye that isn't swollen shut.

Salmon of Knowledge

"Ah, lassie, it's like Balor you look with his one terrible eye. Let your Uncle Finn have a look at it."

At the sight of the giant stranger approaching, Tess grabs a branch twice the length and width of her arm and holds it aloft. "Come one step closer, you blackguard, and I'll beat your bones into corn meal mush."

"Easy there, lassie," laughs Finn. "You're liable to hurt yourself swinging around that big stick."

"I mean it," she shouts, bracing herself to strike.

"Tess, no," cries Svana, running over the rise, carrying the healing leaves just in time to see the child make a run for Finn while the wolfhound by his side stands his ground and bares his teeth.

"Don't be fooled, Brann, she can do no more harm than a sparrow."

As he throws back his head in laughter, she whacks him behind the knees with all her small might, bringing him to the ground where she smashes the side of his head. The dog leaps on the child, knocking her to the ground, holding her down with his massive paw.

"Tess, what have you done?"

"Gave him the same I'd give any stranger, coming at me

BOOK THREE

with a vicious dog."

"Brann's no more vicious than an old woman's lap dog. It's you that's frightening."

Finn stirs as the wolfhound crosses to him, licking his face, and Svana lifts his head onto her lap, tapping his cheek.

"Sabd?"

"Finn, are you alright?"

His eyes flutter open. "What happened?"

"You scared the child."

"Child is it? It was more like a hurler bashed my head as if it were a *liathrod* he was slamming beyond the goal post. You've a powerful clout for a lass."

"I know." Tess nods until she groans with the pain of jostling her own bruised head.

"Will you look at the pair of you? I don't know who to apply the leaves to first."

Finn sits up in the patch of bright green ferns and reaches into the inner pocket of his coat. "You needn't waste your medicine on me. Luckily, I filled my skin with a good measure of Owen Reilly's poteen." Finn holds the deerskin flask above his mouth and pours down a stream of amber whiskey. "Are y'sure, your father wasn't a Fenian?"

"My father is William O'Brien, greater than any man who ever lived. My father fought off twenty of the Queen's soldiers with his pike and will be coming back to Ireland to finish off the rest."

"Where is he now?"

"Botany Bay."

"It's a prison far to the south. The child and her brother plan to sail there to find him."

"If the gods be willing, I'll lend a hand in bringing you to him," he says raising his pouch of *poteen*. "To William O'Brien as brave a man who ever lived or fought for Ireland."

Svana peels and applies the leaves to Tess cuts and scrapes. "Where's Eammon?"

"He went back to the scalpeen."

"Back to the bog? Whatever possessed him to do that?"

"I told him to."

"But, Tess, why?"

"I can't sleep without mammy's blanket. She gave it to me. Her own Mammy made it for her when she was a baby. He said to tell you not to worry because if anyone was out looking for him, they'd be on the road to Cork as Thomas told them that was the way we'd be traveling. He made us this fire before going and said to cook the fish."

He examines the fillets of perch and trout. "Ah, and fine fish they are. I'll show you how a Fenian cooks them. Wrap these in some damp oak leaves."

As Svana follows his instructions, with a flat piece of slate he digs a hole into which he tosses fist-sized stones. "It was a pit nearly as wide as Lough Arrow the Fianna dug and filled with as many stones as are atop Knocknarea. Over that we laid one hundred salmon wrapped in sedge and over that another layer of smoldering stones to make as fine a feast as ever was had in County Kildare."

"So, you're partial to salmon then?"

"Aye, for surely you've heard of the Salmon of Knowledge?"

"No, but I've a feeling you're about to tell us," says Svana already accustomed to Finn's love of telling his own tale.

Finn drains the last drops of drink from his skin and tucks it back into his pocket. "It was in ancient times that King

BOOK THREE

Cormac Mac Art was wandering through the *sidhe* when he saw beside the ramparts of a fairy castle, a shimmering cascade. From it flowed five streams, each one making a murmur more melodious than any harpist ever played. Now before the waters parted to go their separate ways, there was a pool so deep no rock dropped down had ever hit the ground. And it was in that bottomless pool that five salmon swam, and at its edge grew nine trees that blossomed all the year round with crimson flowers and purple nuts. And when the hazelnuts grew heavy, they fell from the branch to be swallowed by the fish that spat out the shell and swallowed them whole.

As Cormac sat transfixed by the pool, a maid came to drink the water, and it was her the King asked the meaning of these strange sights. The girl told him that he had come to the Well of Knowledge and the five streams were the five senses that feed all wisdom, and that a sip from its source would bring any Irish man or woman who drank it the great gift of inspiration."

"What if someone ate the fish?"

"Whoever ate the fish that swallowed the nut could bypass all need of study for that lad or lass would instantly become wise in all subjects."

"It's only the stories my Mammy told me of Dagda and Lugh and our own ancestors that I believe."

"Did your mother ever speak of Finn MacCool?"

"No."

"Then, Tess, it's only a part of the story you've heard, for Finn MacCool was a descendant of Lugh himself. And it's him would be your Uncle Finn as well."

"What was so special about him?

"Finn like his father Cumal before him was the leader of the Fianna. Now don't tell me you've not heard of the Fianna?" Tess shrugs and Finn shakes his head in disbelief. "It's an education in your own people you'd be needing from *Finegas* himself."

"Who's Finegas?"

"I'm getting to that. Finegas was the tutor of Finn MacCool, who one day caught a Salmon of Knowledge and gave it to young Finn to cook for him over the fire. Now Finn did, but when he was turning it over on the hot iron, he burnt his thumb on its crackling skin, and it was when he brought that thumb to his mouth like this," says Finn demonstrating. "He received all the knowledge of the salmon himself."

"Was Finegas angry?"

"Not at all. He was as kind and generous a man as ever walked the green earth, and he let me eat the entire fish myself."

"So then, you're Finn MacCool?"

"Aye, Tess, I am."

"I don't believe you, prove it!"

"Come with me to the water," he says leading them to the stream where he leans over the bank. "Now think of a question."

"What kind of question?"

"Whatever question pops into that rock-hard head of yours."

"What's taking Eammon so long?"

Finn places the tip of his thumb beneath his teeth and stares into the water. "Is he a thin sort wearing a ragged pair of trousers held to him by a rope at the waist?"

"That's him." Tess leans over the water but cannot see the

images revealed only to Finn in its shadowy currents.

"Then it's him I see beside my roan mare. His hands are being bound before him by a burly man, and off to the side is a foppish looking gent in a frock coat with a red vest beneath."

"That's Lord Kavendish for sure. And the ganger. Where are they, Finn?"

"I see only a fence and a long drive."

"That leads to the manor house and the stables behind. We've got to go to him, Finn."

Finn whistles once and the Fenian's mare trots to him. Hoisting Tess up, he mounts with Svana behind him, and they ride swiftly across the fields and back to the high-road. The sun grazes the hillsides, casting long shadows across the landscape, as they race down the road where only a day before Svana approached the carriage of Lord Kavendish.

By the time they reach the estate thick clouds have rolled over the countryside and heavy droplets of rain splatter the long drive that leads behind the manor house to the stable. Finn dismounts and hands the reins to Svana.

"Lassie, wait here with the child."

"But I want to fight, too."

"Surely, Tess you'd be a match for any man. But stay here by your cousin." Finn throws his leg over the low stone wall and follows to where men's voices can be heard behind the stable.

"I want to fight with Uncle Finn," Tess insists, sliding off the saddle running to catch up with him. Svana follows down the drive on the Fenian's black mare, pulling back its reins when Eammon comes into view. Just as Finn described his hands are bound and he is astride the roan mare. What Finn hadn't seen was the noose dangling from the branch above his head and resting like a necklace across his collarbone.

"Let's bring these festivities to a close," slurs Lord Kavendish with a nod toward the Constable who slaps the horse's haunches just as Finn steps forward to grasp the mare's bridle and strokes her muzzle.

"Steady, girl."

"How dare you interfere," snarls the landlord who unsteadily crosses to the mare raising his riding crop to strike her into motion.

"Steady, girl," he coos to the horse again as he reaches out and grabs the stick that he snaps in two and tosses aside.

"You meddling, Paddy. Remove yourself from my estate before I have you taken away in irons."

"You insolent fop. It's my people's land, and you are the squatter."

"Seize him," Kavendish orders the ganger and Constable who throw themselves on Finn. The three men grapple on the ground as Thomas comes running across the field, and Svana rides to Eammon's side to remove the rope from his neck while Tess grabs a spade from the stable.

Watching with amusement, Lord Kavendish reaches for a clay jug of poteen as Tess raises the spade by its wooden handle and brings the steel end down on the ganger's head. Eammon leaps from the saddle of the roan mare and lifts the semi-conscious body to deliver a punch to the face while Finn pins the Constable to the ground and raises a boulder-like fist above his face.

"Don't kill, me. I'm an Irishman!"

"You don't smell like an Irishman," replies Finn, knocking him out with one blow.

"You Irish are fond of fists and pikes, but they've never

BOOK THREE

been a match for powder." Lord Kavendish takes his pistol from his waistcoat and takes aim at Finn.

With the spade in her hand, Tess comes behind him and strikes him hard behind the knees bringing him to the ground. With a flash the pistol fires and Finn falls back with his hand to the chest where the ball has lodged.

"Uncle Finn," cries Tess, smacking the landlord in the head before running to his side where Svana, Thomas and Eammon gather around their fallen friend.

"It's spears and arrows I've pulled from my own side, but that's the first time I've ever been hit with one of those buggers," says Finn, reaching into the wound with two fingers and prying out the lead ball. "Bit of a jolt, isn't it?"

Lord Kavendish looks on with horror as the shot man strides toward him bleeding from the chest.

"Sure, a bit of Norman ingenuity's not enough to put down an Irishman." Finn bends over the quaking gentleman and tucks the lead ball in the pocket of his vest. "That's just a little parting gift, and sure but wouldn't you want me to have something in return," he says, snapping up the gold watch on its fob that dangles from his pocket.

"Not the watch."

"Aye, the watch."

"But it's an heirloom."

"These hills are heirlooms, and the day's not long off when their rightful owners will reclaim them. Meanwhile, let's just consider this partial payment of your rent."

"You're a dead man," rasps Kavendish.

"Some would say immortal." Finn tosses the watch to Tess who catches it in mid-air as he reaches for the clay jug of *poteen* at his feet. "And now for a parting drink."

Finn takes a swig of the whiskey and then bracing up the limp body on the ground, he pours the rest down his throat until it gurgles up like a stream and the gentleman falls back in a stupor. Thomas runs to Finn's side and shakes his hand warmly.

"Whether it's Finn MacCool or Finn the Madman you are, you have our thanks."

"A debt easily paid by taking care of these two young Fenians. Though watch out for the lass, she's a wicked temper."

Tess smiles broadly.

"That I will gladly, Finn."

Crossing to a puddle, Finn places his thumb under his tooth and studies its surface.

"Then go with them to Dubh Linn where at the quay you'll meet an agent for a ship called the Lark that will take you south."

"Will we find my dah?"

"That I cannot see. My intuition only tells me you will struggle on that continent, as there the English dog us out the same as here. But in the future our descendants will fare well, for in any free soil the Irish always prosper."

"But what if he wakes and calls for the soldiers."

"We'll set you on them, lassie, and free the whole country," replies Finn as the friends laugh.

An evening mist has settled over the road. "Don't worry, lassie, this cloud will cover your way."

"Take the horses," says Finn picking up Tess and placing her on the back of his mare, "but leave them at the hurdle bridge when you come to Dublin and they'll find their way back to the Fianna."

"God be with you," replies Thomas who takes hold of the reins and rides off with Tess down the long drive.

Eammon puts his arm around Svan's waist and pulls her close to him. "Are you sure you won't come with us?"

"It's here in Ireland I have to stay."

He kisses her long and hard on the mouth "Then I'll be back."

"They'll be boarding the ship before you're through there, lad."

Eammon releases her and mounts the Fenian mare. "I will be back."

"And whatever world I land in, I'll be waiting."

As he rides off toward Dublin, Svana, flanked by Finn and Brann, walks east toward Tara.

White-Sided Tara

As the mist over the fields thickens, Svana walks slowly, surveying the ground to be sure a patch of earth will secure her next step. For whether she is coming to the edge of a lake or a cliff or the edge of the earth itself she cannot tell, so thick are the churning coils of fog.

"Finn, are you sure this is the way to Tara?"

"How certain can I be when every time we turn, a century has passed. But, aye, in my day all high-roads led to Tara, running through the five provinces like veins to the heart of Ireland. And unless I've been flummoxed by the fairies, this is the road that ran along the coast from Bray to Dublin then westward straight up the slope of Tara where soon we'll see her high white walls and the smoke rising from the Great Banqueting Hall. That is if this *fe-fiada* ever lifts."

"What's fe-fiada?"

"You're walking in one, lassie, it's the same fe-fiada that will keep your friends safe from the view of their enemies until they board their ship at the quay. The same cover that fell over the Tuatha when first they came to this island, hiding them from the sight of the Firbolg until they could set up camp and defend themselves. And it's the same phantom cover that conceals their fairy forts from mortal eyes, parting only on Samhain when unsuspecting mortals can tumble through."

"Too well I've learned that lesson."

Suddenly through its thinning strands Brann leaps, barking wildly as the ground beneath them trembles. "Steady, boyo, easy."

Finn strokes the wolfhound and tries to calm the girl who clings to his arm. "If the earth opens, Finn, don't let it swallow me. For I can bear any world so long as the light of day moves across its fields."

"It feels less like the ground opening than an army moving towards us," Finn replies as the first battalion of silent soldiers cross their path.

Two, four, six abreast they come: a legion of does and fawns. She and Finn stand, the waves of the deer formations passing by them like the parting currents of a stream. "How will we know her?"

"By her eyes. They're not the dark globes of these creatures, but each one a bright isle floating on a foamy white sea. You'll not miss them for they're the same as Oisin's."

Svana's gaze moves from doe to doe until the last of the herd of hundreds has passed and the earth beneath them becomes still.

Finn casts his eyes downward. "Destroyed I am with looking."

"Don't lose hope now, not when what you seek is a glance away."

"Sabd," Finn utters, peering through the gauzy mist where a woman comes to him from across the road. With her skin and cropped hair the color of a fawn, her oval face and bare, shapely limbs, Sabd embodies all the grace of a deer in a woman's body.

Silently she approaches Finn and greets him in the ancient

manner, resting her cheek on his chest. Finn inhales deeply, enveloping the slight woman in the folds of his great coat while Svana stands close by, admiring the gentle slope of her back.

"Our son?"

"Oisin is safe with the Fianna."

She smiles, shivering in the cool moist air that beads on her skin while Finn takes off his coat and holds it open to her. She slides her thin arms into its cavernous folds, and Finn laughs at the sight of her with its sleeves dangling down to her knees.

"Sure, you look like a tinker, but the prettiest tinker I've ever seen."

Crossing to Svana, she kisses her three times on the cheek as the last veils of the Fe-fiada are lifted by a warm wind, revealing atop a high hill, the curving ramparts of a fort. "White-sided Tara," murmurs Finn.

"It looks as if it were carved from one great block of stone," marvels Svana.

"That is *Rath-Righ*, the fort of the Kings and there to its side is the Great Banqueting Hall."

Even from this distance, the boldly carved and painted structure dominates the landscape. Long enough to house five hundred huts with its roof of red oak shingles gleaming against the backdrop of a cloudless sky. Then from the rooftop sounds a trumpet blast that rolls down the hillside.

"There's the first blast of the horn. That means they're calling for the shanakie to come arrange the hall for a feast this night, for it's only the historian of the Tuatha who knows where to seat each chieftain, king and warrior. We came on a good day, lassie, for these are always grand affairs."

Even more wondrous to Svana than the halls of Tara is the

sight of the thousands of Irish women, men and children gathering on that hillside as abundant and radiant in their bright, flapping silks as wildflowers in a field. Yellow, crimson, blue, checkered, striped and boldly patterned, their mantles flutter in the breeze as they move and out of the canopied tents. Her eyes dart up and down the slope, her mind reeling at the complexity of pleasures mingling there. Before her are harpists, clowns and equestrians riding bareback, standing astride their galloping horses whose ears have been dyed red while their purple tails stream behind them. Bakers hawk their trays of cake and trifle while two men who hold branches with bells above their heads chant lines of verse.

"Who are they?"

"They're poets matching wits. The one recites some line of an ancient verse or invents a few lines and challenges the other to complete the poem on the spot." Applause rises from the place where the two poets compete while on the grassy plains below the sloping lawns surrounding Tara, others gather for the games and races.

One group throng around an oval track where behind the painted posts handlers hold back their greyhounds. Further off a roar rises from a playing field as the *liathrod* is thrown up into the air between two teams of players, and when it falls, the men battle for it with their curled sticks of ash.

"The hurling's begun. Can we go, Sabd, can we go watch the game?"

Svana giggles to hear the warrior pleading like a boy to run off with his mates. Then from the crowd stumbles a haggard looking man on whose shoulders rides a black-haired toddler. Around the child's chubby fists are twisted two long tendrils of the tired Fenian's beard, reins which he whips vigorously while kicking hard to urge his weary stallion forward.

"Finn, you've returned! Take the baby, man. I'm begging you, take Oisin!" At the sight of his mother the baby grows still. His green eyes mist over as if the sadness of their parting has only just occurred to him. His lower lip swells and quivers. Tears rolling down his cheeks, he reaches out, flexing his fingers eagerly to be held by her.

Taking the hefty baby in her arms, she sits on the grass and pulls back the lapel of Finn's coat. Oisin ducks under the flap and feeds hungrily until a woman passes, carrying a curly blue lap dog. With a yap the dog jumps from her arms and runs past the nursing baby who pops out his own curly head and shouts, "*Oirk!*"

Oisin then leaps from his mother's lap to chase the pup through the forest of legs followed by his fretful parents.

"C'mon, laddies," the liberated Fenian calls to his comrades who have been sitting in a circle close by, smoking their pipes and lounging around a wide, smoldering pit. The men are passing around the four handled *medar*, each man taking a swig from a squared corner until the wooden vessel is drained. They then hurry down the hill toward the game with Svana close behind.

While the Fenians make their way through the crowd of onlookers that stand ten deep, Svana finds a vantage point on the hillside where she watches a short, powerfully built athlete dominate the playing field, fending off all challengers from the liathrod before bashing it into the gap between two bushes that have been clipped into a goal post. And when Lugh raises his clenched fist into the air, half the crowd curses and jeers while the others shout their praise to the champion,

BOOK THREE

none more loudly than the young woman whose waist-length silver hair flies about like the mane of a stampeding mare as she claps and stomps and whistles from where she stands watching on the slope.

Sneaking behind, Svana grabs Holly around the waist, ducking down to hide, forcing the good witch to twist and turn, trying to catch sight of her.

"By the smell of you I know that you're a mortal and that before the feish this night begins, it's a hot bath you'll need, daughter Dé Dannan." Holly spins around and tackles her young friend to the ground.

"For all the ages that you've traveled, it's still you've kept my sprig of golden bough in your hair."

"More than once it's been the hope of finding you that's kept me from despair. Is everyone here?"

"Not everyone. At least not yet. But Dagda is waiting for you. He made me promise I'd bring you to him straight away."

Taking hold of her hand, Holly leads her up the hill. When they pass the peaked tent with the royal blue and blood red stripes, Svana stops, startled to see the silver shadow of Nuada's hand emerge and pull open the flap. Peeking in, she sees the backs of a hundred heads over which the hand floats, beckoning for her to follow.

"What's going on in there?"

"Shush!"

An angry spectator silences her. Rising on tiptoe she enters and stands on the edge of the crowd beside Holly, trying to catch a glimpse of what holds the audience's rapt attention. In the crowd a burly, red-faced man, whose cheeks appear to be on the verge of bursting, gives up his place in the front row and hurries down the aisle, trying to choke back the coughs that rack him when he reaches the open air. Through the space he vacates, she sees two robed men intent on their game.

On the lacquered board of black and white squares the players have positioned their opposing armies—one of yellow gold, the other of white bronze. Beside the board, King Nuada's Silver Hand lies useless. The King strokes his beard with his flesh hand as he studies the board, unaware that the spirit of the Silver Hand hovers above the game. Svana watches as it dips and merges with the metallic hand of the King. Inspirited, the Silver Hand rises from its inert position on the table.

"Ah-ha," exclaims Nuada, realizing his next move, as rejuvenated the Silver Hand grasps a rider and stallion, moving three squares toward its opponent who sits back in his seat, viewing the maneuver through a tiny slit beneath the lid of his single, bulging eye.

"That's Balor!" blurts out Svana, startling the ogre whose raised knee sends the pieces hurtling across the board and onto the rushes that cover the floor.

"Who dares disturb our game!" howls the giant rising to his feet.

"Sorry."

"Who are you who distracts kings from battle?"

"I am a girl from Sligo."

"A peasant girl at Tara?" asks King Nuada stepping forward. "How did she get past the fe-fiada? It's not till sunset this night the eve of *Samhain* that a mortal may pass through."

Holly steps forward. "She's no peasant, but the Northman's daughter, the daughter De Dannan whose arrival we've awaited." The crowd's suspicious glares at the intruder fade and their eyes are bright with recognition of their own.

"Then you are very welcome, for you have been sent by Danu herself to close the gap between the worlds of legend and the living, bringing our tale to a close and with it the cycle of blood and vendetta, heralding the beginning of an eternity of peace for the Tuatha." Nuada places the Silver Hand on her shoulder.

"It's thanks to her arrival that you and Nuada can now fight over *fidchel* at Tara instead on the shore of Lough Arrow."

"Then, Holly, truly she is a welcome guest. For it's not easy for one as old as myself to keep taking that stone through the head time and again. Not now that age has taught me better."

Two blasts of a trumpet sound from atop the Great Banqueting Hall. "They're calling the shield bearers to the Hall, so that each shield can be hung on the wall above the place that each shall sit. It won't be long before we are all summoned for the feish. Excuse us, now," explains Holly. "I must take the girl to the *grianan* with the women to prepare for this night, farewell."

"Set up the board!" calls Nuada while the crowd in the tent return to their seats.

"What's the grianan?" asks Svana trying to keep up with Holly.

"It's a special place for the ladies in *Rath-Righ*, built in the sunniest corner of the fort. But first we must stop at the Slope of the Embroiderers." They hurry toward the hillside where women sit around table-sized frames, their adept fingers busy with their many-colored threads and needles. Svana tugs at Holly's sleeve.

"Wait. I have to tell you something."

"We have no time to chat now. Save it for the feish."

"But I want you to know it wasn't Danu at all, but Queen Maeve who sent me here. She told me I had to bring her the Silver Hand. And I didn't."

"Nonsense. Maeve may think herself the great goddess, but believe me, you are here by Danu's decree. As for the Silver Hand, clearly it is with its intended owner."

"But will she be there tonight? If she is, I'm doomed."

"Nobody's doomed, girl, only Maeve by her own unrelenting greed."

"Maybe she won't come."

"Whether Maeve appears or not, you've nothing to fear. You are safe in the company of the Tuatha. Now enough chattering. We must prepare."

Svana follows to where the women sit around table-sized frames, stitching intricate landscapes. Drawing closer, her eyes widen, taking in the silky greens and deep blues of the vast landscapes the women embroider.

"That will hang in the Banqueting Hall," says Holly who then leads her to a beam from which hangs a pale blue linen dress, its accordion pleats inspirited by the breeze that fills its myriad folds. Across its bodice and hem white stitches swirl and flower, creating a wreath of babies' breath and lilies.

"It's beautiful. Just like in my dream. The same as my father brought for me from Dubh Linn when I was little."

"It's yours," says Holly as one of the embroiderers steps up on a stool to take the dress down from its hook. Svana reaches out for it, but Holly drapes it over her arm. "Oh, no you don't. You're not to touch this dress until you've had a hot bath."

But her attention has already been drawn from the flowing fabric of her gown to the intricate weave of aromas that waft

BOOK THREE

from a steamy red tent—the smell of meat, leeks, mushrooms and spices. Stepping into the outdoor kitchens, she watches the men and women up to their elbows in flour who beat and knead dough while others at a table, their knives a blur, chop the leeks and mushrooms while still others with stone pestles and mortars grind spices. At the hub of this commotion stands Dagda, stirring the Cauldron of Undry.

Svana slips behind him and taps his elbow.

"The flies on this hillside are driving me mad," he complains, brushing away her tiny hand.

"Dagda, it's me."

Dagda sets aside the oak branch with which he stirs the stew and turns to face his visitor who he grabs and lifts high above the cauldron. "Oh, lassie, I'm so glad you're back. You don't know how I've fretted over you. Are you hungry?"

She inhales the fumes from Undry that moisten her cheeks. "Dagda, it's half-starved I've been with missing you,"

"Brother," booms the voice of a man even taller and broader than Dagda himself. "Let my niece come to me!"

"Ah, will you give it a rest, Goibniu. She's only just got here." Dagda sets her down on the ground between him and his brother whose forearms are like saplings and his chest a landscape of sleek muscles. First he grips Dagda's hand until his brother winces though he tries not to show it. Then he opens his palm to Svana who rests her own hand that is but a tiny rose bud in his.

"It's a pleasure to meet you, niece."

"The pleasure is mine, uncle. I asked my grandmother about you many times."

"It was your line that kept the brooch safe all these generations."

Svana's stomach clenches. The brooch, she lost the brooch that morning on Lough Arrow when she left it and her purple blanket on the boat that drifted out onto the lake. How can she now tell him that she lost so precious a family heirloom?

"Uncle Goibniu? I've something to tell you."

Dagda, standing behind his brother, puts a finger to his lips before stepping forward.

"Not to worry, lassie. Goibniu will understand. You see, brother, it was to me she gave the brooch for safekeeping before heading over to the Field of Tears for fear of it being lost in battle."

Dagda opens his hand to display the shimmering brooch, which he pins to Svana's mantle as Holly gives her a wink.

"Uncles, we must take our leave now until tonight. Besides I'm sure you're busy with your own preparations."

"Aye," says Dagda, sniffing the air. "What's that burning? Can I not leave the side of Undry without the stew being ruined?" Dagda berates the first chef who is unlucky enough to cross his path while she heads off with Holly and her uncle Goibniu.

"It's him that's been getting absent minded in his old age. Why just this morning he cooked the porridge until the currants were black and Undry so burnt it took ten young squires to scrub out the inside at the Well of Nith."

Goibniu motions for them to follow him into a cream-colored tent that houses row upon row of oaken casks. From a shelf lined with gleaming chalices, he chooses the smallest one that he holds delicately between his thumb and finger. Tilting its rim beneath a spigot, he lets the amber liquid flow into its silver depth. He hands it to Svana.

"I want you to sample tonight's míd."

BOOK THREE

"I don't mean to disappoint you, Uncle, but it was just a sip of the poteen that I had, and I didn't like the sensation at all. And since I've been tossed about from age to age, I'm not sure my head can bare anymore spinning."

"Not to worry, lassie, that poteen's of another age altogether. My míd is a much milder, sweeter brew. It's the drink we always offer our guests when they arrive. A thumb's measure for a lady."

He hands her the silver cup engraved with concentric rings. She raises it to her lips and sips the míd that is as aromatic as honeysuckle. Its light sweetness rolls over her tongue and flows down her throat, filling her with a gentle warmth.

Svana drinks from the cup, noticing how the rim of the Goibniu's cup casts a gleaming circle on the white top of the tent. "And, look, it does glow with the light of dawn."

"Aye, when it's the likes of you drinking from it."

"We must hurry now," urges Holly.

When they step from the striped tent, a loud snort greets them. It is the wild boar whose once-sad eyes now glint with the joy of their reunion. Svana crosses to her bristly old friend and strokes his snout while he nuzzles her affectionately. His mate, Bridey's pig, comes running to join them, scratching the ground with her cloven hoof.

"Not to worry," says Bridey who comes up behind her. "She's just a bit jealous. You know how it is with newlyweds."

Before Svana can reassure the boar's bride, she is nearly toppled over by a stampede of wild baby boars, snorting and snuffling loudly. "Yours?" she asks her old friend who nods proudly as a tiny gray runt of the litter, its eyes barely open, rams into her ankle and keels over on its side.

She picks up the handful of gray bristles as it opens its

eyelids and sets its dark gaze on her. "Oh, he has your eyes," she exclaims to the boar who then looks to his bride. She nods her assent.

"They want you to have him. As a gift."

"Oh, Bridey, I do love him, and I'll keep him always," she says nuzzling him with her nose.

The piglets run squealing down the hillside with their parents close behind as Holly takes her hand and they run toward the vast white wall of Rath-Righ. Its massive carved oak doors are open as members of the Tuatha hurry in and out. Within the walls are two more circular forts and the many wickerwork dwellings that dot the sunny green *lis,* mown and weeded so that it feels like a carpet.

Cradling the infant boar who has fallen asleep in her hands, she follows Holly to where the sun shines down on a dome-shaped building of polished hazel rods thatched with the feathers of a thousand birds: sleek stripes of reddish purple, blue, yellow, red and brown encircled the roof of the grianan. Holly pushes open the carved oak door opening to a central room where women lounge and chat on low couches. Then moving on, she parts the silk drapes to another small compartment. There stands a canopied bed with four polished pillars connected by rails from which tea-colored lace curtains hang from gleaming copper rings. Across its feather filled mattress is spread her purple blanket.

"But how did you get it?"

"You are not the only battling swan I've befriended on this lake. In the distance I saw the lovely white bird pulling it along, and I watched it approach the shore where it laid the blanket and brooch at my feet. I recognized them both as yours."

"Thank you," murmurs Svana, holding the fabric to her cheek. "And its color is still true,"

"For it was dyed with a thousand whelks," replies Holly as she reaches toward a narrow table top that extends from a leather couch on which a glass bowl has been set, brimming over with creamy custard. "This is for you."

Svana dips in the small golden spoon and tastes the sweet brechtan.

Holly pulls back the curtain that surrounds the steaming copper tub. "This is for you as well. But hurry, the third blast will sound at any moment."

Svana sets down her new pet on the cushion where it snores, flexing its small legs in its sleep as if he were still running down the hillside. She crosses to the platform of slate tiles and steps up, pulling her cloak and shift over her head and hanging them from an iron hook on the oak beam. Dipping her foot slowly into the fragrant, soapy water she feels a wave of relaxation overtake her as she lowers herself into its warmth. Her pleasure is soon disrupted by the tug of Holly's brush through her snarled and twig-entangled hair, yanking and pulling until sleek tresses hang over her shoulders.

She intertwines the sprig of Golden Bough into the five-stranded braid that she weaves down her back, clasping it with a gold ball.

"Holly, why me?"

"What do you mean, child?"

"Why did Maeve send for me?"

"Maeve was only doing the bidding of the great goddess of the Tuatha, Danu who intends to end the bloody battles and bring the tales of the Tuatha to a peaceful conclusion. But to arrive at that place at the end of time, we needed a bridge between the land of legend and the living."

"But why me?"

"Because you are of the last living line of the Tuatha Dé Dannan."

"But I know others will follow for it's my own descendants who befriended me."

"Yes, but another mortal could not have navigated the misty terrain without a phantom guide, and it was your father who was summoned from the Other Side to lead you to Lough Arrow. Without him, you'd have been lost forever in the fe-fiada."

"So, it wasn't solely for myself I was chosen, but because I am the Northman's daughter."

"Yes, but to reach Tara you had to choose to follow him."

"In the beginning I only followed him out of fear."

"But at Lough Arrow you forgave him, and it was then by choice you followed him to the Cauldron of Undry."

From outside the grianan come the sounds of a scuffle. "Invader in Rath-Righ! Invader in Rath-Righ!" Holly crosses to the small pane of glass that looks out onto the lis. "It's a Northman," comes another cry as three trumpet blasts sound from the rooftop of the Great Banqueting Hall.

"Hurry," she says bringing a thick white sheet to Svana who has already jumped dripping from the bath. "It's your father."

She dries herself quickly and pulls the new dress over her head as Holly tosses a pair of white leather cuaráns at her feet which she slips into hurriedly. Outside the solarium a current of excited curiosity runs through the crowd that parts when Lugh steps toward the center where two guards wrestle with

BOOK THREE

the intruder on the ground.

Svana pushes through the gawking onlookers to reach her father where Lugh has pulled off the guards.

"Release him."

"But, Lugh, he's a Northman."

"Yes, he's a Northman, but he's one of us. Good to see you again, Father Bones." He extends his hand, glistening with jeweled rings, to the man entrapped in his daughter's arms. He rises with her clinging to his chest.

"And a pleasure to find you all again," replies the Northman.

"Come," calls Dagda, running with some difficulty toward the entranceway of the rath. "Everyone is already inside."

With Lugh beside them, Svana and her father are leading the stragglers from Rath-Righ and across the hilltop toward the Great Banqueting Hall when suddenly Svana turns back, running toward the fort.

"Where are you going?" her father calls after her.

"I forgot something," she shouts, running all the way back to the grianan and into her own compartment where she finds her pet boar happily wallowing in the bowl of custard, licking its glass wall. "You're the one who needs a good scrub now."

She dips the boar into the soapy tub, then wrapping him in her purple blanket, hurries to her father who waits to accompany her to where the Tuatha has gathered.

The Last Guest

With the swaddled baby boar bouncing up and down in her arms, Svana keeps pace with her father's long strides as they pass through the gates of Rath-Righ to the Great Banqueting Hall. "Have you ever seen so long a house? If a cock crowed at one end, you'd not hear it from the other."

At each of the six massive doors that line both sides of the Great Banqueting Hall, nine men put their shoulders to the heavy oaken planks. "Hurry," calls Holly, "all are seated and awaiting your arrival."

Inside, iron lamps hang from the vaulted ceiling like gargantuan spiders dangling from black filaments, and although the sun has not yet set, all have been lit. The candle flames cast wavering shadows across the long tables that line each side of the hall where on the walls hang the shields of the warriors who sit beneath them. Some are wickerwork covered with hide, some whitened with lime while others of wood are painted red-purple and brown, ornamented with gold and silver rivets, some short as a forearm and others long enough to cover a man.

The Hall stirs with the excitement of the hundreds of guests settling into their seats, calling their greetings down the table to old friends. Chieftains and their wives and warriors sit at long oaken tables, facing the center of the vast room where another table has been laid with the feast: platters piled high with joints and choice slices of beef, lamb, badger and pork; trays of boiled goose eggs festooned with sprigs of water cress; bright pink salmon poached and served on silver plates. Glass bowls heaped high with mounds of yellow cheese and butter dot the table where baskets of steaming loaves of bread fill the air with their sweet, fresh baked aroma.

Beside the gleaming golden plate and goblet of glass set before each guest are two little silver dishes, one filled with salt and the other with honey for dipping, as well earthen pitchers that the servers frequently refill with home brewed míd and ale. Overwhelmed by the abundance Svana stands by the door peering in.

A hush falls over the hall. All eyes turn to follow the steps of a hunched and blind old man led by the hand of a little girl whose yellow hair is festooned with ribbons while behind them walks a boy who carries a triangular shaped, otter skin case. Svana creeps along the edge of the crowd and ducks under a table to get a better view of the small procession that approaches a cushioned seat at the front of the hall where King Nuada sits flanked by his wife Macha and Lugh. Among the company at the King's table sit Dagda and Goibniu. All watch intently as the laces of the hide case are undone, and the gleaming, bowed frame of a stringed instrument is placed in the crooked fingers of its master.

With the first sweet note plucked from those glistening brass strings, the infirmities of age disappear from the musician. His fingers become brisk and agile, and the crags and creases in his face fade, softened by the bright and rapid notes that rise from his harp. The lightness and complexity of his harmonies mesmerize the guests, so that even when the last note dissolves, all sit for a moment, silent in the delight of having heard such a song.

Nuada stands, raising in his Silver Hand a drinking vessel made from the hollow horn of a bullock, studded with gems. "To the harpist," he cries, a toast taken up by all who raise their glasses and drink to the musician's health. "Brothers and sisters, husbands and wives, to all of the children of the Tuatha. It is thanks to the arrival of our own daughter who guided by her father the Northman has braved great hardship to span the bridge of time to link our legends to the land of the living, so that tonight we gather to celebrate not the false victories of war, but the true victory of peace."

The King raises his goblet again and scans the table, staring at the empty seat beside Lugh with consternation.

Whispers run up and down the hall.

"Where is the girl?"

"Call for the shanakie, for he arranged the seating."

"Aye, Lugh," says the historian of the Tuatha who approaches the front of the hall, "I had intended her to sit by you, but where can she be?" Two gentle strands of snoring rise from beneath a table where Svana and her baby boar, doze, drowsy from the centuries over which they have shuttled.

"It seems she's been lulled to sleep by the harpist," says the shanakie who gently shakes the girl's arm. "Wake up, lass. Now you haven't come this far to miss a feast that rivals my own wedding, the one I told you of back in my cabin."

Svana stirs and opens her eyes. "Owen Reilly?"

"Aye, child, I'd not have missed this feish as it may be the last fine tale to tell."

Drawing Svana from under the table, he leads her to her appointed place beside Lugh and Holly.

BOOK THREE

"Where is the girl's father?" asks Lugh, scanning the room until he sees him at the far end of the hall. "Father Bones, come take your place beside us for you are an honored guest."

Svana's father makes his way toward the king's table where he takes an honored seat to the applause of all assembled. As the clapping fades, a rumble rises from the back of the Hall where the massive doors of Tara open and the warriors of Connaught stream down the aisles led by a woman whose swirling silver hair tumbles over her shoulders, shouting, "Since when does a Northman sit at the head table of Tara?"

A noble man rises, grimacing with anger and motioning for her to sit down beside him. "Maeve, not here, not now."

"I will not be silenced, Alill."

"You may be the Queen of Connaught," says Lugh, "but perhaps for once you should bend to the wishes of your good husband and take your seat."

"I'll not join a table with him at its head."

"You may have conjured the bones from hell," says King Nuada rising, "but he and his daughter are here at Tara, not to do your bidding, but to celebrate an end to the ancient wars and the arrival of a new age of peace."

Upon seeing the Silver Hand reattached to Nuada's wrist, Mauve shrieks, "Treachery!" Her rage echoes through the Hall where all sit shocked, unaccustomed to such outbursts at so high an occasion—for according to the law all guests must remain civil, with even age-old enemies calling a truce for the duration of the feish.

"His brutal deeds must be punished. He is one of them. Those who enslaved our own. I for one will not forget."

"But then can you not like the girl forgive?"

"Never!"

Maeve raises a fist toward the warriors of Connaught who shout their support. "Long live Queen Maeve!"

Lugh turns and reaches behind his head where from an iron hook there hangs a long chain heavy with clusters of silver bells. Vigorously he shakes it.

"Lugh has rung the *slabra éstechta*," shouts Macha. "There must be silence in the Hall."

"The law provides for peace at this table where the Feish of Tara must proceed without conflict or dishonor," says Lugh his eyes locked with those of the Queen of Connaught.

"It is you, Lugh Lumfhada, who brings dishonor to Tara by disavowing our time-honored ways of war and retribution."

"It is you, Maeve who dishonor this assembly, claiming to care for the Tuatha when in fact you'd wage any war to satisfy your savage pride and greed." The Dé Dannan applaud his words, but again Lugh shakes the chain to silence the Hall.

"I will be heard," screeches Maeve over the ringing.

"Silence, Maeve. Perhaps you can whip your husband into submission with your nagging tongue, but you'll not dominate this feish, for it is written that whoever transgresses the law of the assembly must die."

"Then kill the Northman for it is his presence that creates conflict. Wipe out the enemy now."

"And make an orphan of the girl?" asks Dagda.

"Give her to me to raise as my own at Ushnaugh, truly the only court worthy of a daughter Dé Dannan."

Holly rises from her seat and crosses to where Svana sits, placing her hands on her shoulders. "Why not let Svana decide?"

"Choose then—be the daughter of a Queen, or a daughter of the bones."

BOOK THREE

Her small voice rings out through the Hall. "I choose my father and my friends."

Queen Maeve's face quivers as she turns toward the door. "Come, Ailill."

Her husband shakes his balding head. "I'm done with your bullying ways, Maeve. I'm staying."

"Warriors of Connaught, follow me!"

They look first to the Queen and then to Ailill.

"Choose now," King Nuada instructs them. "Will it be Maeve and her eternal appetite for wars fueled by your own blood, or stay with the Tuatha to protect an everlasting peace?"

"Sit down, lads," says Dagda, motioning to a long empty table along the side of the Hall. "The feast has just begun, and it's only cowards who turn their backs on Undry."

Unable to resist the goodwill of Dagda, the men take their places among their comrades as a shriek louder than the banshees' cry rises from the red-faced woman at the far end of the hall.

"You've never been more than a war mongering shrew, Maeve, and you won't be missed," says Dagda. "Doorkeepers, let the Queen of Connaught out."

"You can keep your pretense of peace," she snarls back at him. "But you've not heard the last from me."

"It's no doubt I have of that, Maeve," calls out Dagda. "For small hope is there in this world or any other of harnessing that legendary mouth of yours." Maeve grows white with rage as the hall rocks with laughter.

"Likewise small hope have I," said Lugh, "that we'll silence news of the wars you wage beyond our borders over bulls, jewels or oil to light the lanterns of Ushnaugh. You'll turn good people from their own hearths with false promises of greatness and lies about loyalty, when in fact once we join your ranks, we've forfeited our lives and denied our children a parent for the sake of your arrogant pride. Unwittingly we choose death—until the day we teach every child to say no to the slavery you call freedom. Until the day all have left your ranks to join us in peace at Tirnanóg."

Maeve stares with malevolence at all assembled.

"Mark my words, all of you, Maeve is not so easily mocked. And you, daughter of the bones, you failed at the one task I set for you. You scorned my kind intentions. So instead of accepting me as mother, you have made an enemy of me for all time. Silver Hand or no, I will wage my wars and fuel them with the blood of your offspring."

The Silver Hand of Nuada points toward the doors of the Great Hall that creak open.

"Enough, Maeve, be gone from Tara forever!"

"I will go, Nuada, but be sure I will be back. And not for the Silver Hand—next time it will be for your skull." Maeve turns and storms past the guests and out the heavy doors of Tara.

In the silence that fills the assembly in her absence, the metallic snap of the King's fingers echo, signaling the musicians to begin. First the rumble of the bodhrán reverberates through the hall, followed by the interchange of ecstatic fiddling and skirling pipes. With another metallic snap, Nuada summons the stewards who stand in the doorway, waiting in white aprons with silver platters by their sides. With another snap of his fingers, they swarm the feast-laden boards at the center of the Hall, piling them high with the delicacies they then deliver to each guest: thick chops of pork and pungent stewed apples, skewered lamb grilled with wild onions, glistening fish and roasted wild birds stuffed with mushrooms and pungent spices.

All through the afternoon and early evening, they replenish the pitchers, making their rounds until every succulent joint of meat and every trout has been served, every basket of bread emptied and every side plate of honey wiped clean. Even as the sun fades from the high windows, they keep serving trays of sweet trifle and frosted cakes until the very last bowl of creamy custard and honeyed fruit is set down before Dagda whom the entire company cheers on, knowing that only he can consume another bite, which of course he tucks away easily, washing it down with a goblet of míd.

When only a few sprigs of cress and parsley remain on the wide wooden boards, the stewards carry them out of the hall to make room for the entertainment.

First enter the jugglers and painted clowns, their ears rounded with gold rings that gleam in the candle light. The jugglers toss plates and platters across the Hall and towards the rafters, then swords and shields. Then to the raucous delight of even Balor, they add to the swirling mix Lugh's legendary slingshot and tathlum, the very weapon that had taken out the ogre's eye each time the phantoms had gathered by Lough Arrow to fight again the Battle of the Plain of Tears.

"It seems when all is said and done," shouts Balor, "the clowns make better use of our weapons than the warriors."

"Never a truer word's been spoken," agrees Owen Reilly. "Nor a tale of the Tuatha so neatly ended."

"Hold your tongue, man," scolds the portly woman by the shanakie's side. "This feish is far from over, for we've yet to do a reel or a jig."

"Who is this woman, and what is this reel and a jig she refers to?" asks Nuada from his throne.

"Pardon, my wife, as she is from another age when it was customary for the assembled guests to engage in a sort of a step together."

"A step together?"

"The jig being a sort of rump-ada, rump-ada, rump-ada while the reel is more of a rumpadidle, rumpadidle, rumpadidle."

"Show us your jig and your reel," commands the King.

"Like we say back home, round the house and mind the dressers!" shouts Maura, and while the musicians play, she and Owen dance a sprightly jig in the middle of the room. First it is the banshees who take the floor and follow their steps, soon joined by all assembled.

"Let it be known for all time," shouts Maura, "It was a lass from Cavan taught the Dé Dannan a double jig!"

The floor shakes with the steps of their feet, and the hall echoes with the music and laughter that fill Tara through the night. But when the pastel light of dawn dabs the horizon that shows through the skylights, Lugh again reaches for the Chain of Attention, and the fiddlers put aside their bows and the dancers take their seats.

"At this time we wish to present a gift to our guest who has withstood much hardship to bring us together, our own daughter."

Three long, curving trumpets blast from the balcony as a line of women from the Slope of the Embroiderers enter, bearing a massive rolled up tapestry. Latching its velvet loops to the hooks that have been placed along the wall, they unroll the length of fabric down one wall of Tara, around its corner, behind the table of the King and down the length of the other. All the guests marvel at the skill of the embroidery, but none more amazed than Svana who walks to where the tapestry begins and tours the hall studying its imagery.

First she comes to a dome-shaped hut where a full moon hangs over the sea. A few steps further the silk threads portray a girl on a rock with a crested wave rising behind her while on the shore a hooded figure is stitched in black. Svana marvels to see the tapestry show her own story, every episode of the journey from the arrival of the *banshees* on their herd of wild boar and then the vortex of floating bones. She wants to linger at each image, yet feels the urge to see the next pulling her forward. There is Maeve seated atop the cairn of Knocknarea, and next Lough Arrow comes into view where a girl holds a skull above the skeleton that genuflects before her. There are Camog and Skein of Kesh Corran, leading Lugh into the mouth of the cave.

When she comes to where Dagda sits, she turns to him and smiles. "Dagda, look. It's us sitting around Undry. And there's Bridey and her pig."

"Aye, it's all here," Dagda says tenderly tapping his heart.

The images of the Plain of Tears do not disturb her for she knows now that the sounds of that brutal battle will never again be heard. But the sight of the half-starved woman and her child on the road still saddens her.

"I hope they're all well," she says turning to Holly. "And that Eammon and Tess are safe."

Holly takes her hand and leads her past where smoke rises from a scalpeen on a bog, past a stream where a girl's slip floats about her like a lily as she stretches out her arms and swims. They then pass the panel that depicts the fray at the estate, with a small girl wielding a spade about to strike a gentleman whose pistol is aimed at Finn MacCool. There just beyond the scene of Finn handing the reins of his horses to Thomas, Holly points to a ship sailing on a calm sea. On its bow in tight stitches appears the word 'Lark' and on its deck passengers can be seen.

"You see, they will gain passage, and though it will be a hard journey, they will land safely."

Now King Nuada rises and with another snap of the fingers of the Silver Hand all the warriors rise and take up their spears.

"What's happening?"

"With the dawn this feish shall end with the clashing."

"Clashing of what?"

"Listen."

A rhythm echoes through the hall with each warrior rapping twice on the table with the end of his spear and then striking once the raised spear of the comrade beside him. Twice on the table, and once to the side. Twice on the table and once to the side, the accelerating beat conveying an urgency as the time draws near for the conclusion of the feish.

Svana still has a long wall before her, and wanting to catch a glimpse of how her own story will end, she hurries along. Past the silky form of a naked woman emerging from the fog, past the tumult of colors that capture the festivities she witnessed on the hill that day. Past the tents of Dagda and Goibniu, past a stampede of little boars.

"There, you see your brothers and sisters?" she whispers to the little animal that stirs in her arms. "And that's you," she says pointing to the bristly creature depicted climbing into the custard bowl. "But what happens in the end?" she muses,

BOOK THREE

hurrying until she sees only a depiction of an empty Banqueting Hall and then a final panel on which there is only a well bright with green water.

Suddenly a chill wind from the open doors whips through the Banqueting Hall, lifting and flapping the pleats of Svana's skirt, filling her ears with a sorrowful moan. But when she spins around, she sees that not a single phantom remains.

"This isn't fair! You can't leave me. Not after all I've gone through to get here."

Still clutching her baby boar, she hurries past the barren tables, the patter of her leather soles punctuating the silence of the abandoned hall. Through the oaken doorway she runs out onto the hillside, where huffing and puffing a portly woman comes over the rise.

"Has the feish begun yet, a ghrá?"

"It's over, and all the guests have gone away but me."

"Sure, but old age does be so wearisome. All yesterday I sat thinking to myself, Danu, there's some place it is you've promised to be, but for the life of me, it wasn't until this very hour it came to me old fool that I am. Tara, I'm to be at Tara today for the living daughter has arrived."

"You're Danu?" utters Svana shocked that the great goddess of the Tuatha is more wrinkled and forgetful than her own grandmother.

"Aye, a ghrá, and who is it you might be yourself?"

"I'm Svana."

"And aren't you the same sweet child I'd been on me way to meet? Why the pleasure's all mine. Watch your step there, a ghrá," the goddess says firmly planting her freckled hands on Svana's forearm and giving her a quick shove.

Too surprised to utter more than a gasp, she falls back a

step and feels a slick hardness between her foot and the ground. She hears the crunch and leaps aside to see the last jolt of life run through the body of a chalky white snake that lies in the grass, the same hideous snake she had seen slither off into the dark caverns of Kesh Corran.

"Was that Camog and Skein?"

"Good riddance to the pair of them," says Danu, reaching down, whipping back the long dead serpent and flinging its remains over the hill. "Sorry to have taken you off guard, but we've waited so long for legend and the living to merge, and for one of your kind to put an end to that hideous pair."

Svana's blue skirt billows in the breeze that bends the green grasses swirling at their feet, and she recalls Harte's promise that at the end of time the peasant girl would crush the head of the snake, bringing peace at the end of time.

"So, is it the end of time we've come to?"

"Endings are funny things aren't they, a ghrá? So much like beginnings that one can hardly tell them apart. Here your arrival has bridged the ancient times with the land of the living, and our Tuatha is finally free to set aside the swords and slings of the old stories, taking up a life in a land of peace, but who's to say how that will go, eh?"

"Where are you all going, what land of peace?"

"Why, Tirnanóg, the land of peace and plenty where all time converges. Didn't Maeve explain any of this when she asked you on this journey?"

"Asked? Queen Maeve? She didn't ask, she ordered."

"Didn't she tell you, lass, why the Tuatha wanted you here and how all our destinies for all time would converge?"

"Maeve wanted only the Silver Hand to keep the Irish wars raging for all time."

"Well, thanks to you, she's not succeeded in that."

"But what of the Silver Hand?"

"None but the tide will direct the Silver Hand again."

"I don't understand, and I'm tired of riddles."

"You shall see, a ghrá, you shall see."

"I don't see, and after all I've been through, I deserve to know!"

"It's really quite simple. There was a time when life and legend were one in the same. Lugh was a living, breathing warrior, Dagda, the greatest trencherman who ever walked the island. Around each one spun the legends, but being but mortals their time came to an end and with every generation life and legend split further apart, and the tales were tattered and told only in pieces, never coming to an end. Even our wildest warriors became weary of fighting battles in a war that never ended. So it was a living daughter Dé Dannan we sought who could bridge life and legend and bring the tales of the Tuatha to a peaceful conclusion."

"But what of Maeve?"

"In every age there are deceivers, who at the cost of all others, amass greater power and wealth thinking they will rule for all time, but like Maeve they are always undone. Undone by their own greed and finally by the people grown weary of the wars."

"What am I to do?"

"It's all been worked out, and I really must get going." The aged but hearty goddess leans over and kisses her cheek three times.

"Wait, you can't leave me here."

"The folds of time have parted, and I must hurry along."

"Stop!" shrieks Svana.

Danu turns at the door of Tara beneath the carved lintel and regards her calmly. "You do realize, that I am chief goddess, and I'm quite unaccustomed to being shouted at."

"It's unaccustomed I am to being tossed from age to age and abandoned on a hillside far from home."

"It's been a pleasure really, but the Tuatha is waiting."

With one step Danu passes through the wavering grain of the wooden door as from the other side a muffled voice adds a final admonition.

"And remember, a ghrá, do not fear the Glistening!"

Holding the tiny boar close to her chest with one hand, Svana takes hold of the wooden knocker and bangs angrily. But with each rap the rampart fades until nothing but the boulders at its foundation remain at her feet.

"This isn't fair. You have each other, I want my family back," she screams, stomping on the ground.

Fiercer than her tantrum are the winds whip about the fading walls of Tara. Svana scans the hill for shelter. On the northeast slope there flows a sparkling stream that darkens as the slate gray clouds pass overhead, and a jagged wind tears the hazelnuts from the tress at its edge. When a frantic togmall half leaps, half flies past her toward the grove, Svana follows, knowing he is in the same pursuit of safety. And when the creature dives into a trunk and then reappears chattering from an upper branch, she hastens to the hollow hazelnut tree.

Crawling on all fours, she draws her muscles inward to fit through the aperture that seems to her as narrow as the eye of her grandmother's bone needle. From the rotted tree trunk she watches the wind whip up the waters of the well that feed from the stream of *Nith*, and the speckled salmon that leap wildly from the turbulent water.

BOOK THREE

Huddling in the hole, she clutches the baby boar and waits for the pummeling winds to pass. When finally the wailing ceases, she looks out and sees the waters of the *Well of Nemach* have settled. She surveys the damage of the winds that have pulverized every stone and blasted every timber. Where the halls had stood, no structure remains. The hill is barren except for the long grasses dancing in the green currents that have swept away all but the rocky traces of where the Royal Halls of Tara once stood.

As she crawls from the snug womb of the hazelnut, the little animal leaps to the ground with the tiny boar that wriggles from her arms in swift pursuit. The togmall hops nimbly across the white stones and leaps, clearing the water of Nemnach with ease, but the boar cannot. For an instant it hovers over the gaping mouth of the well before plunging down into the green water that glows with a light from below.

Falling to her knees, Svana peers into the bright rings, mesmerized by the concentric waves that draw her closer and closer until without resistance she tumbles over the edge into the well.

Down, down she falls into the shimmering waters that do not darken with the depth, but grow lighter until the crisscrossing currents shine like the sun glinting off the facets of a thousand gems. Without fear, she glides effortlessly through the watery tunnels, following each turn with ease, luxuriating in the gel-like touch of the cool water against her skin.

Moments, maybe eons pass, and still she travels the watery byways while all memory of her previous journey fades, both of her life among the living and her adventures among the gods. When she comes to a dark chamber of cold water, she tastes its saltiness on her lips and feels her body rise. Her face breaks through the surface, and like a newborn with no trace of experience written across her mind, she gulps her first breath of the mussel scented air.

For a moment fear rises within her, drawing her downward, when beyond the breaking waves, a pair of swans and two cygnets paddle toward her. At the sight of them, her muscles, recall the movement that now keeps her skimming along the surface of the sea beyond the cresting peaks where the waves break and fan out along the shore.

Spreading her arms outward, pushing aside the frigid water and firmly kicking her legs strengthened by the countless miles she has traveled, she swims toward the shore where men and women are gathering. Behind them on a grassy hillside, she sees the thatched rooftops of their cottages whose circular white walls are tinted with the shifting shades of a salmon dawn.

A low wave overtakes the swimmer, tumbling her like a stone and rolling her out onto the sand at the feet of the villagers.

From the crowd an old woman hurries toward the shivering girl who emerges naked from the surf. Pinned to her shawl, a brooch gleams with a blue stone. In her arms she carries a homespun blanket, dyed a rich shade of purple that she unfolds to wrap around the girl's glistening shoulders. Over the dunes runs a woman with long copper hair, followed by a tall, fair haired man with a close-cropped beard.

When he bends to lift the dazed girl, a glint of silver catches his eye. From the bubbling surf he fishes out the Silver Hand and holds high that ancient relic of war. Then as he hurls it past the breakers and it sinks into the sea, a joyous cry arises

BOOK THREE

from the people. His then lifts and carries the dazed girl down the beach while a small boy with thick black curls trots alongside them.

When they pass a low stone hut, a bent man in a hooded cloak emerges and smiles, making a motion with his bent fingers from his head to chest and crossing himself over his heart, kissing his fingertips, and nodding toward the early morning procession. The old woman who wears the ancient brooch passes arm and arm with her daughter and nods back toward him, wishing the holy man a good day.

Not far behind the procession scurries a wet baby boar. No bigger than a sod of turf, it shakes the sea water from its bristly hide as it runs, following the villagers down the beach and over the embankment to the old woman's cottage.

The neighbors linger in the yard, peeking under the leather flaps that cover the portals in the cottage wall, watching the Northman lay down his daughter on a bed of hides as his wife unfurls the doeskin over her. By the fire the boy who crouches beside the grey wolfhound blows hard on the dying embers until the sods crackle and fill the cottage with their earthy smell. It is then the baby boar zig-zags through the thicket of legs and startled feet that jump aside as he hurries across the yard, beneath the cow skin that hangs over the doorway, diving under the doeskin blanket to nuzzle against the drowsy girl. The villagers' laughter overlaps with the notes of an ancient song that rises from the cottage, where two mothers sing to the girl who sleeps peacefully unaware of all the worlds she has traveled or that the name of the one in which she has landed is Tirnanóg, the world where forever she will be at home.

Timeline

For mythical, legendary and historic events that relate to *The Northman's Daughter*.

c. 1015 BCE The end of the reign of *Tuatha Dé Dannan,* who retreat after their defeat to dwell on the Other Side.

750 BCE The first (mortal) *feish* convenes at Tara.

c. 100 AD Queen Maeve of Connaught wages war against Ulster.

c. 177-297 AD The legendary *Fiana* defends Ireland.

432-461AD As Bishop, Patrick spreads Christianity throughout Ireland until his death.

c. 560 AD The final (mortal) *feish* convenes at Tara.

793 AD Viking raids along the coast of Ireland begin, leading to the Norse settlement of *Dubh Linn*

Timeline

845 AD The Viking *Turgeis* captured & executed by drowning with a stone around his neck by Malachi, King of Ireland.

982 AD Svanhildur, child of Irish-Norse origin, born in Sligo to a son of Turgeis and a descendant of the *Tuatha Dé Dannan*.

995 AD Svanhildur stumbles through a *fe-fiada* and shuttles between the lands of her ancestors and her descendants.

1170 AD Anglo-Norman warriors invade from the island of Britain.

1695 AD The Penal Laws, enacted by the English invaders, deprive Irish of their cultural and civil rights.

1845 AD The failure of the potato crop and the beginning of the Great Hunger and the Irish diaspora.

Glossary

a ghrá (**ah graw**) Irish term of affection, love or my treasure.

Ailill (**ahl**-il) after marrying Queen Maeve became the King of Connaught.

Balor (**bahl**-or) the one-eyed tyrant who ruled the *Fomorians*, the monstrous sea gods said to inhabit Ireland before the arrival of the *Tuatha Dé Dannan*.

banshee (**ban**-shee) "women of the *shee*" who with their men folk the *fershee*, retreated after the defeat of the *Dé Dannan*, beneath the hills of Ireland to dwell in their diminutive form; also believed to align themselves to families, wailing at the onset of death of its members.

bechdin (**bek**-din) in Old Irish "little bee house" and in a land where the condiment was in constant demand, meals were served with a small dish of honey to dip fish, meat, bread or vegetables; houses, rich and poor, kept their own hives.

Beltene (**bel**-tin-a) "bright fire" the first day of *Samhradh* (summer) in ancient Ireland, our May 1st, when fires were lit throughout the countryside to enhance fertility of the cattle and insure good fortune in the coming season.

bodhrán (**bow**-rawn) hand-held frame drum, played with a double headed tipper, resonating with a sound like distant thunder.

boreen (**bohr**-een) Anglo-Irish word for a little road or country lane.

boreen-brack (**bohr**-een brak) "speckled cake", the sweet loaf prepared with currants and served on eve of *Samhain* with a ring or coin baked into the dough as a symbol of good luck.

Botany Bay a brutal penal colony in Australia, established by the British government in the late 18th century where many thousands of Irish men, women and children were exiled for petty crimes, to clear the land and provide labor for the overlords.

bratha (**brah**-ha) "a twinkling of an eye", which according to one ancient text measured two minutes and twenty-four seconds, a very long twinkle.

brehon (**bre**-hon) one of the learned class of men versed in Irish law, history and poetry entrusted with the interpretation of the law and passing of judgments.

Brehon Law legal system of ancient Ireland that evolved over hundreds of years of custom and usage as recorded by the *brehons*; this code regulated all aspects of civil, criminal and military law, defining and protecting rights of all classes of

Irish society from kings to slaves, managing all aspects of property from building to bee-keeping.

Brigid (breet) daughter of *Dagda,* goddess of poetry and known for her protective care, whose birthday is still celebrated on the first day of Irish spring, *Imbolc,* our February 1st.

Cauldron of Undry a great bronze pot owned by the god *Dagda* from which friend and enemy alike were fed; only cowards refused to partake of the stew from Undry which never emptied.

Cian (**Kee**-an) respected member of the *Tuatha Dé Dannan,* brother of *Goibniu,* who stole into the crystal tower on Tory Island to court *Ethlinn* (eh-leen), imprisoned by her father, the tyrant *Balor.*

cloghan (clo-**kan**) bee-hive shaped dwelling of stone where some monks resided in a solitary life, removed from the monastery.

Connaught (**kon**-acht) one of five ancient provinces of Ireland: Connaught, Leinster, Munster and Meath; subdivided into territories, the smallest being the *tuath,* land occupied by a tribe.

Cuchulainn (coo-**hool**-in) son of *Dé Dannan* warrior-god *Lugh,* champion of Ulster, according to the Ulster cycle of tales, legendary for his strength, daring and at times his anger, whose life was cut short by the treachery of Queen Maeve in

Ulster's battle against Connaught.

Cumal (**ku**-mal) "sky", legendary leader of the *Fianna* and father of *Finn MacCool* who succeeded his father, leading the band of warriors to its height of fame.

cuarán (**cur**-awn) leather slipper or sandal.

curragh (**kur-**ah) a boat with wickerwork sides and ribs covered with cowhide, tanned oak bark and tarred at the joints, light enough to be carried over land.

Dagda (**dagh**-da) the "Good God" also known as *Ruad-Rofhessa* (roo-ro-essa), the Lord of Great Knowledge, the beneficent chief of the *Tuatha Dé Dannan,* legendary for his appetite, as well as the abundance of his Cauldron of Undry from which he fed foe and friend and only cowards walked away unsatisfied.

Danu (**dah**-noo) the chief goddess of the Irish, worshipped for the abundance of her good nature, whose name is remembered in *Da Chich Anann* (the Paps of Danu), two beautiful hills in County Kerry.

Diancecht (**Dee**-an-ket) famed physician of the *Tuatha Dé Dannan* and god of medicine whom legend credits with having attached the silver hand to *King Nuada*, maimed in the first Battle of *Moytura*; however, when his own son *Miach's* words, brought the hand to life, *Diancecht* became so jealous that he murdered him.

dillat (**dil**-lat) thick embroidered cloth over the horse's back used by the noble classes of Ireland, often covering the entire animal.

dirna (**dir**-na) a weight in ancient times, thought to have been between one and six ounces, a *dirna* of silver could purchase a white cow.

dolmen a single portal megalithic tomb constructed of two upright stones on which a large flat stone was set.

Dubh Linn (**doov**-lin) Black Pool, this ancient Celtic site was claimed by the Vikings, not for its riches, but for the accessibility and defensibility of its location on the River Liffey.

duilesc (**dil**-esk) a sea plant that grows on rocks and in ancient times whose harvest and consumption was regulated by Brehon Law.

Errach (**arr**-ock) the season of spring, which according to the ancient calendar began on Imbolc, February 1st.

Ethlin (eh-**leen**) daughter of *Balor*, who fearing the prophecy that he would be slain by his grandson, locked her away in a crystal tower on Tory Island where she was sought by *Cian*; by him she gave birth to three sons, only one of whom survived; the orphan Lugh was rescued and raised by *Goibniu*.
fe-fiada which concealed it from mortal view; also known as a magical fog as hid the approaching *Dé Dannan* from the eyes of the *Firbolg* when they first landed on the shores of Ireland.

feish (fesh) a feast or celebration which applied to three great social meetings held in ancient Ireland, the largest convening at Tara every three years on *Samhain*, where for several days there were feasts, sporting events, music and various entertainment, as well as the discussion of important business, including checking of historical records, making new regulations and proclaiming the laws.

Fer-liath (fir-**leeth**) the "gray man", believed by some during the Great Hunger (1845-48) to have caused the blight that killed the potatoes and caused the famine.

fershee (**fir**-shee) "men of the shee", the male counterparts of the *banshee*, the former *Dé Dannans* who retreated to dwell under the hills of Ireland for all time.

Fianna (**fee**-ah-na) band of Irish warriors whose tales occupy the netherworld between history and legend, whose greatest achievements are assigned to the reign of Cormac Mac Art (254-77 A.D.) under their leader Finn MacCool.

fidchell (**fih**-el) a game of cíal (kee-al) attention and fáth (faw) judgement played on a board of black and white squares with hand carved pieces depicting kings and their entourages; chiefs took pride in their *fidchell* boards and pieces, decorating them in precious metals and gems.

Finegas (**Fin**-e-gas) aged seer, poet and tutor to young Finn MacCool who after having caught the Salmon of Knowledge gave it to his student to cook; but when Finn burnt his thumb on its seared skin and sucked on it, gaining some of its knowledge, Finegas generously gave the entire fish to the boy who he deemed worthy of its wisdom.

Finn MacCool or *Finn MacCumal* son of *Cumal* who led the *Fianna* after his father's death; Finn surpassed all previous leaders and with the goddess *Sabd,* granddaughter of *Dagda,* fathered *Oisin,* the greatest poet of all Ireland.

Firbolg (fir-**bolg**) or "bag men" this legendary race of Irishmen predated the arrival of the *Dé Dannan* who defeated them at the First Battle of *Moytura* although their warrior Sreng MacSegain lopped off the hand of King Nuada thus forcing him to give up his throne.

*Fomorians (**fo-moor-ee-ans**)* according to Irish myth these early inhabitants of Ireland were often depicted as having only one eye, one arm and one leg; led by the tyrant Balor, they were defeated at the second Battle of *Moytura.*

Gale Day On May 1st &/or November 1st farmers paid the rent to landlords.

geasa (**gesh**-ah) in ancient Ireland certain actions were believed to bring misfortune; a taboo as determined for kings as well as other classes of people, that prohibited certain actions.

Goibniu (**goy**-nyoo) the magical smith and much renowned brewer of ale of the *Tuatha Dé Dannan*; brother of *Cian,* he rescued his abandoned nephew *Lugh* to raise as his own son.

grianan (**green**-an) among the noble classes of ancient Ireland women had a separate apartment or structure constructed in the sunniest area of the homestead.

Imbolc (**im**-bolc) originally *oimeld*, derived from *oi* (sheep) and *melc* (milk), signifying the first day of ancient Irish spring, February 1st.

Kesh Corran located in County Sligo the caves, reached by a steep 200-meter climb, which according to legend once housed the mythological Three Hags of Winter, in this story portrayed as Camog, Skein and Holly.

Knocknarea located in County Sligo this hill, 327 meters high, is topped by a huge flat-topped cairn which according to legend contains the tomb Queen Maeve.

liathrod (**lee**-road) in ancient times, the ball used in the game of hurling, about 4 inches in diameter, made of tightly woven yarn and covered in leather which was struck by a carved stick of ash toward a goal between two posts or two bushes.

Lughnasa (loo-**nah**-sah) "the games of Lugh" signifying the first day of autumn, our August 1st as the day when people gathered for the most important athletic events of the year.

Lugh (loo) a member of the *Tuatha Dé Dannan,* revered both as a warrior and worshipped as a god; also known as *Lugh Lamfhada* (of the Long Arm) probably due to the decisively shot stone from his sling that killed *Balor* and won for his tribe the Second Battle of *Moytura.*

Maeve (mayv) the ancient warrior-queen of Connaught most famous for her attack on Ulster and the death of the hero Cóuchulainn; her name is commemorated today by the *Mioscin* Maeve, the cairn atop Knocknarea in Sligo that bears her name.

Macha (**mock-**ah) wife of *Nuada* and warrior who is slain at the Battle of *Moytura.*

Moytura (moy-**tir-**a) "Plain of Tears" the site on Lough Arrow where the legendary battles between the Tuatha *Dé Dannan* and first the Firbolg and then the Fomorians took place.

Mamó (**mam-**owe) grandma

Manannán Mac Lir (man-ahn-**nahn** mock-**lir**) the sea god whose name derived from the Isle of Mann in the Irish Sea who drove a chariot as easily over the waves as across the fields.

Mecon (**mak-**an) in medieval times the tap-rooted vegetables, particularly carrots and turnips, staples grown in most kitchen-gardens.

míd (**meed**) fermented drink made chiefly of honey, less intoxicating than ale, but considered more of a delicacy often served to guests in a thumb's measure.

medar (**meed**-ar) a communal drinking vessel with two or four handles that was passed around among drinkers.

Miach (**mee**-ak) son of the physician of the *Tuatha Dé Dannan*, *Diancecht*, who surpassing his father's skills, incited his jealousy and was murdered by him; legend tells that from his grave sprouted 365 healing herbs.

mioscán (**mis**-caun) "a lump of butter" also referred to cairns such as the pile of stones atop Knocknarea in Sligo.

Morrigan (Mor-**ee**-gan) goddess and shape shifter who sometimes appeared as a young woman, a withered hag and other times as a bird, usually a crow whose cries preceded a battle and during the fighting could be seen circling overhead.

Nuada of the Silver Hand (Noo-**ah**-dah) a King at the time of the First battle of *Moytura*, he lost his throne when his hand was lopped off by a warrior of the Firbolg, making him according to the Law unfit to rule; the smith *Goibhnu* forged a silver hand which was brought to life with the magic herbs and words of *Miach*.

ordlach (**or**-lok) a "thumb's measure", twelve of which equal a troigid.

oirk (urk) Old Irish for a small lap dog.

Oisin (o-**sheen**) son of Finn MacCool and Sabd, a goddess turned into a deer; when she licked her son's forehead there grew a tuft of fur which accounts for his name, literally, "little fawn"; he became the greatest poet of Ireland.

pinginn (**pin**-jin) by the eighth century silver coins, rough edged and stamped on one side, weighing the equivalent of eight grains of wheat, were used in Ireland.

poteen (pu-**cheen**) very potent, home-brewed Irish whiskey.

praties (**prae**-tees) potatoes

rath (rath) "fort" circular rampart, consisting of two walls separated by a ditch which surround the royal residence of Tara.

Rath-Righ (rath-**ree**) "fort of the kings" which occupied the summit and southern slope of Tara. It was the original fort erected by the first occupiers of the hill, thus the most ancient of all the monuments of Tara.

rán (rawn) spade used in the tilling of soil.

Sabd (saeve) a goddess whom a jealous druid transformed into a deer. When hunting, the Fenians surrounded her, but Finn set her free and was rewarded when she returned to him in the form of a woman; alone she gave birth in the woods to the baby she raised in the wild until he was found by his father who named him *Oisin*.

Samhain (**sow**-in) on its eve, our first of Nov., when the *fe-fiada* around each *shee* dropped, mortals might pass into the land of the fairies.

Samhradh (**sow**-rah) Irish summer which began with Beltene.

scalp/scalpeen (scalp) shelters during the Great Hunger, described in the London Times (Dec. 15, 1849) as a scalp being a hole in the ground 2-3 feet deep used as a rough, temporary shelter while "a scalpeen is a hole, too, but the roof about it is rather loftier and grander in its dimensions" with walls and some rough furniture.

shanakie (**shan**-a-kee) an Irish story teller who was not only a teller of tales, but of history.

shee or sidhe (shee) refers both to the world of fairies and the underground world they inhabit; according to the legend after a two-hundred-year reign in Ireland and their defeat by the Milesians, the *Tuatha Dé Dannan* held a secret council and took up residence in the *shee* where they themselves became gods.

slaan (slawn) tool for cutting turf.

slabra éstecha "Chain of Attention" in ancient times at meetings such as were held during festival of Tara, a chain on which hung silver bells that were shaken to call for attention in the hall.

Slainte (**slawn**-tche) Irish toast to good health.

Slighe (slee) any one of five roads that in ancient times connected Tara to each of the provinces of Ireland.

tathlum (from *lic tailme*, stone of sling) slings and stones were lethal weapons for ancient warriors, who sometimes made their own missiles from a variety of hardened materials. Legend suggests the *Tuatha* had their own magical recipe of blood of toads, vipers and bears, mixed with sea sand.

Tirnanóg (**tir**-na-**nóg**) "land of the ever youthful people" another world of peace and beauty, inhabited by fairies that exist deep under the sea, a lake, well or *shee*.

tógmall (**tog**-ml) a small wild creature mentioned in ancient Irish texts sometimes tamed as a pet and trained to sit on its master's shoulder

troigid (**tro**-id) an ancient measurement equivalent to twelve *ordlachs* or thumb measures.

Tuatha (**too**-a-ha) tribe.

Tuatha Dé Dannan (**too**-a-ha deh-dahn-nuhn) "tribe of the goddess Danu" a mythical race who, according to ancient texts were the fourth prehistoric colonizers of Ireland and brought with them unsurpassed skills in metal working, magic and all the arts and sciences.

Turgeis (**tor**-gis) infamous Viking, feared for the cruelty of his scourges who was captured and executed by drowning by King Malachi in 845 AD.

Ushnaugh (**ush**-neh) royal residence of the legendary Queen Maeve of Connaught.

Valhalla (vol-**hol**-la) in Norse mythology from Old Norse Valhöll "hall of the slain" the majestic chamber located in Asgard, ruled over by the god Odin, the place where half of those who die in combat travel.

Well of Nemnach (**nem**-nok) in ancient times a plentiful well near Tara located on the north-east side of *Rath-Righ*, from which flowed the stream of *Nith;* according to the legend wells, along with other bodies of water, were natural portals to *Tirnanóg*.

Well of Slane (slaun) wells have been venerated as sacred in pagan and Christian Ireland; according to legend the physician *Diancecht*, along with his son and daughter even more powerful in the art of healing, sang incantations over the well, conferring upon it the power to restore the wounded and dead warriors with its sacred water.

Bibliography

A SOCIAL HISTORY OF ANCIENT IRELAND by P.W. Joyce First published in 1903. These two volumes were reissued by the Irish Genealogical Society in Kansas City, Missouri in 1997.

WARS OF THE IRISH KINGS from the Age of Myth through the Reign of Queen Elizabeth by David Willis McCullough, New York: Random House Inc, 2002.

ANCIENT IRELAND FROM PREHISTORY TO MIDDLE AGES by Jaqueline O'Brien and Peter Harbison, New York, Oxford Press, 2000.

BLACK POTATOES: The Story of The Great Irish Famine, 1845-1848 by Susan Campbell Bartoletti, Boston: Houghton Mifflin Company, 2001

HOW THE IRISH SAVED CIVILIZATION: The Untold Story of Ireland's Heroic Role from the Fall of Rome to the Rise of Medieval Europe by Thomas Cahill. New York: Doubleday, 1996.

Acknowledgements

First thanks to my son Ben Ressler who as a boy once told a tale of banshees, floating bones and a wild boar, and who for two years assisted in researching Irish legend, myth, and history for the book we didn't know we were writing. And to Teddy and Momo for listening night after night as the story unfolded, adding their own insights and details.

Thanks to my mother and father, Frank and Frances Merwin, and to our cousin Maura McCaughey who took off her apron and hurried from behind the counter in Shaw's Confectionary in Mullingar to lead us back to the site of the family home in Cavan from which my grandmother Catherine Reilly emigrated in 1905. And to my teacher P.W. Joyce whose remarkable 2 volumes, *Social History of Ancient Ireland* (1903), preserved the life of the land she left behind.

Heartfelt thanks to Berní McGovern Gallagher who first led me up the slopes of Knocknarea. To her mother, Sheila O'Connor-Mcgovern, for pulling out her fiddle the first Sunday I stepped in the doorway, who at eighty-six still plays for the "old folks" in Screen, Co. Sligo. And to Kathleen and Aidan McNally and their children Aidan Og, Conor, Tara, Grace and Joseph for keeping up the unshakeable traditions of Irish family and friendship.

And deepest appreciation to Trevor Lockwood, the Renaissance man of Felixstowe, England who published the first edition of this book in 2005 and has been my devoted friend and literary ally.

Agus is é sin an scéal.